Nannie Belinda and Mr. Pig
by
Betsy Lawrence
Age 6

Please address questions and book requests to: Silhouette Reader Service
U.S.: 3010 Walden Ave., P.O. Box 1325, Buffalo, NY 14269
Canadian: P.O. Box 609, Fort Erie, Ont. L2A 5X3

Born in the USA

Mississippi

PEGGY WEBB

Beloved Stranger

Silhouette Books

Published by Silhouette Books

America's Publisher of Contemporary Romance

SILHOUETTE BOOKS
300 East 42nd St.,
New York, N.Y. 10017

ISBN 0-373-47174-2

BELOVED STRANGER

Copyright © 1991 by Peggy Webb

This edition published by arrangement with Harlequin Books S.A.

® and TM are trademarks of Harlequin Books S.A., used under license.
Trademarks indicated with ® are registered in the United States Patent and
Trademark Office, the Canadian Trade Marks Office and in other countries.

Printed in U.S.A.

Dear Reader,

I was on the Mississippi Gulf Coast when Belinda Stubaker popped into my mind, fully conceived and begging to tell her story. I saw her cheap rayon dress, her outrageous high-heeled shoes and her cardboard suitcase. But more thanthat, I saw her dreams. Like countless women, Belinda longed for a place to call her own, a warm and welcoming place where she could love and be loved.

Place has always influenced my novels, and certainly the stately antebellum homes peering at the Mississippi Sound through curtains of Spanish moss are models for the home in *Beloved Stranger*. I carried Belinda's vision with me to my home in the northeast part of the state and kept it alive when I wrote the book that remains one of my favorites.

Because I wanted Belinda to have the best of everything, I gave her a wonderful hero complete with two delightful children. Betsy and Mark are modeled on my own children, both grown and married now. I still consider my children to be my greatest achievement.

When Silhouette told me that *Beloved Stranger* would be a part of the BORN IN THE USA series, I was receiving the happy news that my son and his wife are going to have their first baby in March. A week later, my daughter and her husband called to say they are having their second baby, also in March. I can't think of anyplace I'd rather my grandchildren be born than the U.S.A.

For Laura Taylor, beloved friend

Prologue

The only thing Belinda had ever wanted was a little house all her own with geraniums on the front porch. What she had ended up with was a pink slip from the Pets and Paws Beauty Clinic telling her they didn't need her anymore to help trim shaggy poodles and clip surly cats.

She stood at the window of her apartment in Augusta, Georgia, thinking about her life. She'd always been traveling from one place to another, listening to the empty promises of men. The first one had been her daddy.

The next town is going to be better, kids. Just you wait and see.

They'd waited and waited and waited. The next town was never better, only farther away. She and her two sisters had remained ever hopeful, though, hanging on their daddy's words and believing.

The believing got harder after her mother left. Looking back, Belinda guessed her mother just couldn't stand the suspense anymore, never knowing exactly where she would be from one year to the next.

Lately Belinda had begun to feel like her mother. She just couldn't stand the suspense anymore.

The reason she was in Augusta was Charlie Crocket. He'd said if she'd follow him to Georgia and help out with the rent till he got his feet on the ground, they'd get married. Well, she'd followed him, and he hadn't lasted in Georgia till the sun got hot.

She knew from the first time she met him that Charlie needed a little straightening out, but she'd thought all it if would take was a bit of patience and understanding. She'd sure guessed wrong about Charlie.

Before him there had been Matt Hankins. He was a beautiful man full of beautiful promises. Just when she'd been ready to pick out the wedding dress, he'd up and joined the army.

Belinda crumpled the pink slip and threw it into the wastebasket; then she took her purse off the couch and counted her money.

She was through being a traveling woman; she was done with suspense. What she was going to do was get on a bus and go as far as her money would take her.

She didn't know where that would be, but she did know one thing. When she got there, she was going to be a new woman—and in complete charge of her life.

Chapter One

Reeve Lawrence lifted his head, listening. The house was too quiet. He shoved his chair back from his desk and headed for the door.

"Quincy. *Quincy!*"

Quincy appeared in his doorway, drying her wet hands on her apron.

"You don't have to holler, Mr. Reeve. I ain't deaf." Her rubber-soled shoes squeaked as they bore her massive weight into his study. When she was inside, she craned her neck to look up at him and shook a finger in his face. "You ain't got no business gettin' yourself all worked up, settin' in here bellowin' like a wounded bull. What's the matter wid you?" She studied the dark circles under his eyes and the lines of fatigue around his mouth. Quincy had been taking care of

Reeve since he was in diapers, and she wasn't about to shirk her duty now.

Her face softened as she reached up to pat his face and smooth down his collar. "You want to have a stroke and die? Then where would them poor motherless children be?"

Reeve grabbed her shoulders. "Where are the children?"

"They out in the yard—running a lemonade stand."

"My children are running a lemonade stand?"

"That's what I said."

"Betsy and Mark are out in the street like two little urchins, peddling lemonade to strangers?"

"I don't know about no urchins, but I know about you." Quincy planted her hands on her hips and faced him down. "You done turned mean since Miss Sunny died. Mr. Reeve, she's dead, and they ain't nothin' me or you either can do about it."

Reeve didn't deny that he'd turned mean since his wife's death. He'd also turned cold, but thank God Quincy didn't point that out. She was getting too bossy in her old age. He probably should let her retire, but she was the only one of his household staff who had remained faithful since Sunny had been gone.

Sometimes he thought of Sunny's death in that way: he pictured her merely gone on an extended journey somewhere—say to the Greek Islands—laughing and tanned in her gold bikini. It was easier than thinking of her in a crumpled car, broken and lifeless.

"You all right, Mr. Reeve?"

Quincy's soft inquiry brought him back to the matter at hand. He put one hand on her shoulder, gently this time, and gave her a sad smile.

"I know I've been asking too much of you, taking care of my house and my children, too."

"Them angels ain't no trouble at all."

"They are rambunctious hellions, and you've worn yourself to a rag trying to watch after them since Miss Phepps departed."

Quincy snorted. "She didn't depart. She hightailed it out of here like the devil hisself was after her."

"I admit her departure was hasty."

"All them highfalutin' women you call nannies has been hasty leavin' here. There ain't no pleasin' you where them children's concerned."

Quincy was right again. Eight nannies had come and gone since Sunny's death, less than two years ago. He'd sent three of them packing, but the other five had left on their own. Miss Phepps, the last one, had called him a dictator. That was mild compared to what the others had called him. The redoubtable Miss Grimes had called him a cold heartless bastard.

"You're damned right I'm hard to please. My children are my life." Reeve ran his hand through his hair, a habit he'd developed lately. "Look, Quincy, I'm sorry I'm such a bear. Go back to your work and don't worry about the children. I'll watch after them."

He strode from the den, a tall muscular man with haunted dark eyes. To the casual observer, he was still a commanding presence, a man whose very walk denoted wealth and power. But to Quincy he was a sad, shattered man, a man in need of a woman's loving touch.

She clucked her tongue as she watched him go.

"It ain't them children I worry about, Mr. Reeve," she whispered. "It's you."

Reeve's children were sitting on the grassy sloping bank at the edge of their front yard, their feet scruffing restlessly on the hot sidewalk and their faces shiny with sweat and hope. A pitcher of lemonade and six paper cups sat beside them on a child-sized folding card table. On the table was an empty shoe box and a sign printed in red crayon on the side of a grocery bag—Lemmonaid, 3 sents.

"Daddy!" Six-year-old Betsy left her position beside the box and catapulted into his arms. "Did you come to buy some lemonade?"

He'd come to take them back into the house where they'd be safe, but with Betsy's hot little face nuzzling his neck, he didn't have the heart to say so.

"That's exactly why I'm here, sweetheart." He sank to the grassy slope, holding Betsy and reaching out to tousle his seven-year-old son's blond hair. "Will you pour me a glass?"

Betsy hopped off his lap and became serious and important as she poured his lemonade. Reeve was equally solemn as he accepted the cup.

"That will be three cents, Daddy," said Mark, obviously the business manager in the lemonade venture.

Reeve passed three pennies to his son and watched as Mark carefully counted them into the empty shoe box. "You're our first customer, Daddy," he added, proud of himself.

Reeve had piles of work on both his desks, the one at home and the one at the office of Lawrence Enterprises. He had a trip to San Francisco in two days and one to Germany in a week.

What his mind told him to do was hustle his children inside to the safekeeping of Quincy so he could get on with his business. What his heart told him was a different story.

He listened to his heart, and he spent the afternoon in the front yard with his children. He and Betsy and Mark discussed whether holes had bottoms and whether ladybugs were really ladies and whether angels flew like birds or like jet airplanes.

Except for Mrs. Clampett from down the street who passed by walking her dog, Reeve was his children's only customer. When the children got anxious over their business lull, he put three cents in their shoe box and asked for another glass of lemonade.

By late afternoon, there was only one glass left. He had decided to buy their last bit of lemonade and take Betsy and Mark into the house when he saw a woman coming up the street, walking almost sideways because of the weight of her cardboard suitcase.

She was dusty and disheveled, as if she'd been walking a long way. He stood up, for there was a dignity about her that made it impossible for him to sit sprawled on the grass, observing her.

When she was two houses away, she stopped on the side of the street, opened her suitcase and pulled out a pair of bright red spike-heeled shoes. Then she sat on the curb and unlaced her sneakers. Her hair fell in a silky curtain over the side of her face, and the setting sun burnished it gold.

Reeve caught his breath. Sunny's hair had been gold. For a moment he was whirled backward in time, seeing his wife as she bent over her shoes, getting ready for the theater.

Suddenly the woman stood up, and she was not Sunny at all. She was a stranger wearing a cheap rayon dress with a spray of artificial flowers at the shoulder, striding toward him in outrageous red spike-heeled shoes.

"I'm just dying for a something to wet my whistle," she said when she was even with him.

He was too astonished to speak. His children didn't suffer the same malady.

"Would you like to buy a glass of lemonade?" Mark said.

"Well, now. I don't mind if I do." The woman fished around in her purse, a large carpetbag affair that was almost as big as her suitcase.

She passed three pennies to Mark, her face as shiny and bright as her red enameled fingernails. There was something heartbreakingly innocent about her smile. As Reeve watched the woman squat beside Betsy, he realized that he hadn't seen a smile that guileless on a woman in a long, long time.

"Well, now," the woman said to his daughter, "if you're not just the prettiest little thing I've ever seen. What's your name, honey?"

"Betsy. What's yours?"

"Belinda..." The woman paused, biting her red lips. "Belinda Diamond," she proclaimed in a voice just a bit too loud. Then she glared up at Reeve as if she expected to be contradicted.

There was something very wise about her dark eyes, as if she were a battle-weary soldier who was coming home with her dignity and her brave red fingernails intact. Reeve was intrigued.

"I'm Reeve Lawrence, Miss Diamond, and these are my children, Betsy and Mark."

Her handshake was spontaneous and strong. She tossed her head when she smiled at him, and the sun shot sparks in her hair.

"You're the first person I've met in Tupelo, Mr. Lawrence." She spoke with careful formality, as if she'd invented the words for the occasion.

"Then you're new here?"

"Brand-new. Just got here this very minute. Left Augusta on the bus early this morning, just me and my suitcase."

"You walked from the bus station?"

"Every step of the way. I don't believe in hitchhiking. Too many bad things can happen to a woman that way."

She smiled again, that unexpectedly innocent smile that set off gold lights in the center of her dark eyes. Then she bent her head over her lemonade.

The children lost interest in the grown-ups and scampered across the lawn, playing tag. Instead of excusing himself and following them, Reeve stayed on the sidewalk with Belinda Diamond, keeping his children in sight.

He had the uneasy sense of having opened Pandora's box. It was unlike him to carry on conversations with strangers, and it was even more unusual for him to be interested in their lives. What was there about this young woman that intrigued him so?

He didn't know. All he knew was that he had to find out why she had walked from the bus station and why she was wearing high-heeled shoes and a dress with artificial flowers on the shoulders.

"Do you have a particular destination in mind, Miss Diamond?"

"I'm headed for the big time. I mean, if a woman leaves everything she has behind except her clothes and she even dresses for the occasion, don't you think she should expect good things to happen?"

"That sounds reasonable."

"You sure do talk fancy, Mr. Lawrence. High-class like."

"Why don't you call me Reeve, and then perhaps I won't seem so lofty."

"Well, if that's not the bee's knees." Her hand shot out again, and she pumped his enthusiastically up and down. "You can call me Belinda, and you'll be my first friend in Tupelo."

How long had it been since he'd had time for friends? Since Sunny's death his life had consisted of managing his business and taking care of his children. The first had been no problem; in fact, it had been his salvation in the long days of grieving. But the second had been a constant battle. With nannies coming and going and Quincy being overindulgent and the children growing and changing every day, his personal life was totally out of control, spiraling downhill like a snowball, growing bigger and more cumbersome with each roll.

Standing there in the late-afternoon sun with Belinda's slim hand in his, he suddenly felt humble and very, very grateful. She made life seem so simple. *Here I am, and here you are,* her handshake indicated to him. *So let's be friends.*

"You are an unusual woman, Belinda." Her hand trembled a little in his, and he self-consciously let it go.

"Oh—you mean the dress." He didn't, but he saw no reasons to contradict her. She smoothed the cheap skirt over her slim hips and patted the spray of flowers. "I've been wanting this dress for I don't know how long. And I just up and decided, why not? Why not get fancied up and go to Tupelo looking like somebody. You know what I mean. Somebody important and *worthy.*"

He found himself gazing into her eyes and not being

able to look away. A dozen things he should say floated through his mind. "You *are* important and worthy," he could say. But she had wise eyes, and probably a wise heart. She'd know he was being shallow. And she had said he'd be her first friend. Real friends were sincere and honest with each other.

"I wish you the best of luck in your new venture, Belinda."

She set the empty cup back on the table, her eyes sparkling. "It's going to be a big adventure, all right, making my place in this brand-new town. See, I'm through being a traveling woman. I'm setting down here for good. Won't that be just grand?"

She smiled at him, and he knew he was being called upon to say something. There were no words adequate enough for Belinda's great expectations. Reeve spent a moment pondering his response, and in the end he merely reached for her hand once more and shook it solemnly.

"Well...good luck," he said. He felt foolish repeating himself, but he need not have worried that Belinda would take offense. She picked up her suitcases, gave him a jaunty wave and started up the street, tilting a little under the weight of all her possessions.

He stood watching her walk away, mesmerized by the absolute dignity of a woman who had so little but still found life so grand.

"Daddy...Daddy!" His children finally caught his attention by tugging on his sleeves.

"How come that nice lady is walking, Daddy?"

"I don't know, Mark."

"Where is she going, Daddy?"

"I don't know that, either, Betsy."

Belinda had reached the end of the block, and as she rounded the corner, the late afternoon sun spread an aura of brightness around her. She looked brave and magnificent, walking off into the sunset in her red high-heeled shoes.

Reeve put Belinda Diamond out of his mind. "Let's clean up the lemonade stand and go inside, children. It will soon be dark."

Mark took the shoe box and carefully counted the pennies into his pockets. Then he lifted his face up to his father. "Is it safe for that lady to walk in the dark, Daddy?"

There was no easy answer to his son's question. He had warned his children never to leave the house after dark unless he or Quincy accompanied them. He had stressed to them the importance of not taking up with strangers. How could he tell his son that Belinda Diamond was a stranger to them, an adult who was responsible for her own welfare, without seeming callous and uncaring? Being told by Quincy that he had "turned mean" was one thing; but being perceived as heartless by his children was quite another.

Before he could answer Mark's question, Betsy piped up with, "What if she gets lost in the dark? Will goblins and haints get her?"

Goblins and haints? He carefully masked the anger in his voice as he bent over his daughter.

"There are no such things as goblins and haints, Betsy. Where did you hear those words?"

"Miss Phepps," Betsy and Mark chimed together.

"She said they come out of the dark to punish bad children," Mark added.

If he had not already dismissed her, Reeve guessed that he'd have killed her.

"Miss Phepps was wrong, children. Goblins and haints do not exist. And there is no such thing as bad children."

"Not even when I put that frog in her bed?"

Reeve stifled his laughter. Mark's prank had upset the entire household, for when she'd discovered the frog Miss Phepps had gone screaming from her room in the middle of the night. Apparently the frog had been content to snuggle under her warm covers unnoticed until she had rolled over on him, pinning him beneath her.

"What you did was wrong, Mark, but it does not make you bad. Both of you are wonderful children. You are my shining stars." He ruffled their hair. "And now, let's finish cleaning up this lemonade business." He was relieved that he had gotten sidetracked from the issue of Belinda Diamond walking alone in the dark.

Apparently the children had already forgotten, as well, for Betsy was carefully stacking empty cups together, and Mark was folding up their grocery-bag sign. Suddenly a bright moisture formed in Betsy's eyes, and she tugged on Reeve's hand.

"But what if she gets scared in the dark, Daddy?"

"Who, sweetheart?"

"That lady with the funny flower on her dress."

His children weren't as easily sidetracked as he had imagined. That knowledge made him both proud and uncomfortable—proud of their bright minds and uncomfortable about having to confront the Belinda Diamond issue again.

She was already out of sight, but she couldn't have gone far, not in those high-heeled shoes and carrying that heavy suitcase. What would it hurt to follow her and offer to take her to a motel in his car? Actually he was a bit ashamed of himself for not already having made such an offer. Had he grown so callous that it took two innocent children to remind him that he was a civilized human being?

"Don't you children worry about a thing. Daddy's going to take care of Miss Belinda Diamond."

"Really, Daddy? Really?" Betsy jumped up and down.

"Yes. I'll go after her in my car and take her to a nice motel for the evening."

"She can stay in my room," Betsy offered.

"That's generous of you, sweetheart, but it's not necessary for her to share your room. Now, let's go inside and find Quincy." He picked up the little table and the empty pitcher and led them back to the house. Inside he summoned Quincy with the intercom.

"Can you hold dinner for about forty minutes?" he asked her. "I have an errand to run."

"He's going after a lady," Mark explained.

"It's about time," Quincy said, rolling her eyes heavenward and cupping her hands in supplication.

"I'll explain later," Reeve said.

He took the black Corvette and went in pursuit of Belinda. She wasn't hard to find. Her shoes and her suitcase had hampered her progress, so that she was only three blocks from his house. He eased to a stop beside her and lowered the car window.

"Belinda..."

She jerked her head around, startled, and then she walked over to him and leaned in the window, smiling.

"This sure is a fancy car." She ran her hands along the edges of the window. "I bet it cost an arm and a leg."

Reeve was momentarily taken aback, then he laughed. "It certainly did. And a couple of feet, as well."

"My, my." She ran her hands lovingly over his car again, all the while leaning so close he was only inches from her seductive little mouth and her dark eyes that seemed to know the mysteries of the universe. His heart kicked hard against his ribs and he was acutely aware of her as a woman. He felt guilty, as if he had betrayed Sunny, but the guilt was only fleeting.

The silence stretched out between them, and Belinda kept smoothing her hands over his car. The movement was decidedly sensual. Reeve cleared his throat and eased back in his seat to put a little distance between them.

"I came to offer you a ride to your motel."

Belinda cocked her head to one side, studying him, holding the moment and offering it up to him like a long-stemmed rose. She seemed to be weighing her options. Suddenly she grinned.

"All right. I'm tired of walking, anyhow."

Reeve got out of his car and loaded her suitcase into the back seat. Belinda slid into the front seat, bouncing up and down a little to test the springs.

"This is just grand," she announced as he slid behind the wheel.

"Thank you." He turned the key in the ignition. "Do you have a reservation?"

"No." Her bow-shaped lips formed a sexy O when she spoke. He couldn't take his eyes off her.

No reservation. And she had already said he would be her first friend in Tupelo. Belinda Diamond was a woman without a friend and without a place to stay. He tore his gaze away from her and faced forward.

"I can recommend a few good motels."

"Are they cheap?" Belinda fingered the catch on her purse as if that small movement would multiply her funds.

Reeve's rescue mission was getting more complicated by the moment. Naturally a woman who had walked from the bus station would be counting pennies. He didn't know how much money she could afford for a motel, and he guessed that if he offered to pay, her pride would be deeply wounded.

"I'll tell you what," he said. "My house is very large and you are welcome to stay for the night."

She didn't seem as surprised by the offer as he was that he had made it. He supposed that was what happened when you started compromising. First he had caved in to the will of his children and become involved in the affairs of a perfect stranger, and now he was letting that stranger work some kind of spell over him so that he was actually concerned about wounding her pride. The Reeve Lawrence sitting behind the wheel of his Corvette was not the man he knew. Perhaps when he got back home he'd be himself once more.

"Is this offer legit?" Belinda asked.

"Yes."

"I don't want you to think I can't take care of myself."

"I don't."

"Or that I go around taking up with strange men."

"Never."

"Or that I don't have any money," she added.

"Not at all." He lied, letting her save face.

"What about your wife? Are you sure she won't mind if I spend the night?"

"My wife is…deceased." Suddenly he had a vision of Sunny sitting beside him, her hair glowing in the dashboard lights. His hands tightened on the wheel.

"Deceased?"

Oh, God. She didn't know what the word meant.

"Dead," Reeve said, his voice tight.

"I'm so sorry." Belinda reached over and squeezed his arm. When he didn't respond, she let go. "It's a deal," she whispered. "I'll stay at your house."

They drove in silence. His house stood out dramatically on the hillside, ablaze with lights. He parked the car in the garage, then got Belinda's suitcase. She fell into step beside him, swiveling her head to view his house from all angles. The children catapulted through the front door and met them in the front yard.

"Daddy, you brought her home!" Mark yelled, obviously pleased.

"Goody, goody!" Betsy squealed.

Belinda stood in front of the house, her eyes big with wonder. "Gosh almighty. It's just like a castle out of a fairy tale."

He looked at his house with a new awareness. It had steep gables and overscaled fanlight. Sunny had added a broad veranda, running the length of the front, so the house wouldn't be so imposing and formidable, she'd said. He supposed it did resemble a castle.

"Do you like fairy tales?" Betsy asked, tugging on Belinda's hand.

"They're my favorite kind of tale." Belinda linked her other hand with Mark's, and the three of them went up the steps together, moving ahead of Reeve.

"Will you read us one?" Mark turned toward Reeve. "Daddy, can she read us a story?"

"That's up to her. She's traveled all day, son, and she might be tired from her journey."

"Oh, I don't ever get tired." Belinda swung around to look at him. "Life's too interesting. If I got tired I'd miss half of it." She smiled at him, then stood on his veranda, surveying her surroundings. "I sure do like this porch," she said after a while, her voice soft and dreamy. "It would be just peachy with two or three big pots of geraniums scattered around."

Reeve imagined his porch abloom with red geraniums. Sunny had loved flowers. When she had gone, it seemed she'd taken all the flowers out of his life, all the color.

He gazed around his veranda. Maybe he'd get some flowers.

"Do you like red?" he asked Belinda.

"It's just about my favorite color in the whole world."

She and the children hurried ahead through his front door, chattering like old friends. He followed along, thinking how it would feel to come home in the evening and be welcomed by red geraniums.

Reeve set the cardboard suitcase down inside the door and reached for the intercom to call Quincy. Then he changed his mind. Suddenly it became important to him to show Belinda Diamond to her room himself. He wanted to see her first reaction.

"Betsy, Mark, please go find Quincy and tell her there will be a guest for dinner." The children raced along the marble floors, laughing and chattering.

When they had disappeared he turned to his guest. "I'll show you to your room."

He led her up the curving staircase, guiding her with a hand on her elbow, watching her openly as she grew big-eyed over the chandelier and the carved mahogany railing and even the plush carpet under their feet. He was as pleased as if he'd invented all those lush trappings.

At the top of the stairs, he turned toward the guest wing, then changed his mind and headed toward his own bedroom wing. There was no need to put Belinda all the way on the other side of the house. What if she need to ask him something and got lost trying to find him? It was much more practical to have her close by. And besides, he wanted to be able to keep an eye on her. She certainly seemed innocent and harmless, and the children liked her. That was always a good sign— children and dogs had great instincts about people.

He trusted his own instincts, too, but there was always a slight chance that he was wrong. It was best all around to put Belinda Diamond in the bedroom next to his.

"Here it is," he said, opening the door to a room done in shades of cream and pale blue. "Your room for the night. It has its own bathroom."

"All of this—just for me?" Belinda swung around to look at him. "You're kidding me. Right?"

"No. This is your room."

She walked around, touching the velvet-covered love seat, running her hands down the silk curtains hanging from the bedposts, picking up the gold hair-brush on the vanity. With the hairbrush in her hand, she suddenly tensed, her eyes as alert as a startled doe's.

"Where's your room?"

"Right next door."

"And where will the children be?"

"Downstairs. My housekeeper, Quincy, has quarters next to theirs."

She laid the brush down carefully, then folded her hands together and faced him.

"I don't swap my body for favors."

"I beg your pardon?"

"I don't know what you think of me or what you expect of me, but I'm not the kind of woman who sells herself for one night in a fancy bedroom."

"I see," Reeve said. She was very serious, and he had a hard time keeping a straight face. He was both amused and touched.

"Just so we get this clear," she went on, "I don't take charity and I don't sleep around—you know, have sex and stuff like that."

He rubbed his hand across his mouth to cover his smile.

"I don't want any of your favors, Belinda, lovely as they might be."

"You don't?"

"No." He opened the closet door and set her card-board suitcase inside. Then he crossed the room and took her gently by the shoulders.

"I'm your first friend in Tupelo. Remember?" She nodded. "What are friends for if they can't offer you a night's lodging?"

She wet her lips with the tip of her tongue. "Okay. I just wanted to make that clear. That's all."

"It's perfectly clear." He released her and stepped back. "Dinner will be served at eight. You might want to freshen up before then. I'll knock on your door when it's time and escort you to the dining room."

She didn't answer immediately, but went to the bed and ran her hands over the creamy coverlet. Her shiny hair slid over her cheek so he couldn't see her face. But even so, he knew just how it would look—as bright and glowing as a child's on Christmas morning.

With one hand, she held her hair back from her face and smiled at him. "I feel just like a princess in a fairy tale."

He didn't know what to say. All he was offering her was a night's lodging. Surely that meager gift didn't make her feel like a princess. Was she expecting more? Was her innocence all an act?

What had he done? He pulled caution around him like a cloak. "I'll see you at eight," he said, already striding toward the door.

She sat on the edge of the bed and looked at the closed door. That Reeve Lawrence was the oddest man she'd ever met. Sometimes he acted all friendly, just like the customers who came to Pets and Paws on a Saturday morning, and other times he was as stiff as an old turkey, waiting for the ax at Thanksgiving. Land, he was a complicated man.

She ran her hands over the coverlet and sighed.

"Oh, Lord, a woman could get used to this." She kicked off her one shoe and curled her toes into the plush carpet. Then she kicked off the other shoe and danced around the room.

Suddenly she stopped in front of the full-length mirror. Her pink dress with the flowers on one shoulder didn't look all that special beside her luxurious surroundings. She was in a different world, and she knew it. Her hands clenched into fists at her sides.

"Belinda Stubaker, don't you dare go making a fool of yourself over Reeve Lawrence. Besides," she added, tipping up her chin, "you don't need another man to straighten out."

Chapter Two

Belinda stood in the bathroom holding a bottle of bath oil. "Attar of Roses," the label read. She didn't know what "attar" was, but she knew about roses. She uncapped the bottle and held it to her nose. It smelled heavenly.

She closed her eyes, imagining herself floating in the big sunken tub, surrounded by rose-smelling bubbles. She couldn't think of anything more elegant.

Sighing softly, she recapped the bottle and set it carefully back on the shelf. Someday she was going to buy herself some bath oil. She'd start with "Attar of Roses" and work her way through the flower garden—honeysuckle, violet, gardenia, daffodil and hyacinth. She might even get some that smelled like spring. She'd have a different fragrance for every day of the week.

Barefoot, she padded back to her suitcase and took out a washcloth and a towel. They weren't plush like the ones hanging in that fancy bathroom, but they were hers. She rummaged around some more, looking for her soap. It was nowhere to be found.

She guessed she'd have to use some of Reeve Lawrence's soap. Maybe he wouldn't mind; and she'd be very particular, using just enough to get clean but not enough to be wasteful.

After her bath she dressed for dinner, then sat on the edge of the velvet love seat, pleating the folds of her skirt between her hands and waiting for Reeve's knock on the door.

She nearly jumped out of her skin when the knock came. She quickly composed herself, then walked toward the door.

Just remember, she said to herself, you're not Belinda Stubaker anymore. You're Belinda Diamond and Belinda Diamond is *somebody*.

Belinda pressed her hands flat on her stomach to still the butterflies dancing there, and then she flung open the door. Reeve Lawrence was standing in the hallway looking like something out of the movies. He nearly took her breath away.

He was dressed up, too, wearing a white shirt that set off his tanned skin and a jacket of raw silk. She knew, for she had once worked in a fabric store.

All at once she was glad she had worn her fanciest dress—the black rayon with red sequins on the shoulders. The skirt flared around her legs when she walked, showing her stockings to good advantage. She was proud of her stockings. They had rhinestone hearts marching down the sides, and they sparkled when she walked. They had been a bargain, too. She'd found them on the marked-down table at a discount store. There was no telling what else she could have found if she'd had the time. But that was back when she was working at Pets and Paws, and she'd been on her lunch hour.

"Good evening." She held her hand out in a formal gesture, the way she'd seen it done in the movies she loved to watch late Saturday nights on her black-and-white TV.

He took her hand just like one of the Hollywood heroes. Goose bumps prickled her arms. Oh, she was going to love Tupelo, Mississippi! Already she was off to a roaring start.

His eyes were crinkled at the corners and his mouth was quirked up when he let go her hand. It was such a friendly look she suddenly felt giddy.

"Look, I dressed for the occasion." She stepped back and twirled around, laughing. When she stopped twirling she could tell by the expression on his face that he'd noticed the rhinestone anklet on her left leg. His eyes were twinkling.

"I can see that you did."

"I added the anklet for a touch of glamour." She twirled again. "What do you think?"

What Reeve was thinking wouldn't do to tell. He'd never seen such an outrageous costume. On any other woman, it would have looked cheap and tacky. But on Belinda Diamond it looked just right, as if she were meant to sparkle from head to toe.

"Well?" Belinda prompted him.

"The anklet definitely adds a lively touch."

"I just knew you'd like it." She came toward him, smiling, and he offered her his arm. Instead of taking it, she slid her hand into his.

Reeve was caught off guard. Her hand was slim and fragile, almost boneless. She laced her fingers with his and smiled up at him in a totally artless way. He felt as if a warm breeze were blowing across the frozen tundra of his soul. At first he welcomed the breeze, for it gave proof that his feelings were not dead. Hard on the heels of the welcome came caution. Sunny was the only woman he'd ever loved: the only woman he would ever love. He wasn't about to mistake his feelings for Belinda for anything except what they were— a certain kind of friendliness for a guileless stranger.

He decided to hold on to her hand a while longer— at least until they had reached the dining room—then he would graciously let her go. In the meantime, he saw no harm in giving in to the pleasant warmth that spread through him.

"I have a confession to make," Belinda said as they descended the stairs.

"You aren't going to tell me you're a cat burglar in disguise, are you?"

"This is serious." Belinda caught her lower lip between her teeth as she looked up at him.

"I'll be serious, then." He bent over her, giving her his full attention. The minute he did so, he knew it was a mistake. There was something magnetic about her face that made him want to lean closer and closer. Her skin was soft and fair, as clear as dew in the morning sun. Her bow-shaped lips were intriguing and inviting. But it was her eyes that held him under a spell. He wanted to plunge straight into those dark mysterious depths, to dive into their shining centers and never look back.

The tip of her pink tongue flicked out to wet her lips. Reeve straightened up as if he'd been punched in the middle. Then he released her hand and moved away from her.

"What is this confession you have to make?" he asked, using his chairman-of-the-board voice.

"I used your soap."

"I beg your pardon?"

"Well...you see, I forgot to bring my soap, and so I used some of yours. Not a whole lot, mind you, not enough to get up a great big lather. But just enough to wash away the travel dirt. A body does get dirty traveling on a bus."

"This is your big confession?"

"Yes."

He was torn between laughter and aloofness. In the end he compromised. His mouth quirked into a smile, but he didn't move closer to her. That was a mistake he wouldn't make again.

"My dear, you may use anything you choose. You are my guest."

"Including the bath oil?"

"Including the bath oil."

"Well—" she thought of the Attar of Roses with a certain longing "—I don't want to be pushy."

"You can be as pushy as you like, Belinda. You'll discover that I'm not a man who is easily pushed."

"Will I?"

Her simple question brought him up short. Of course she couldn't discover his strength nor his stubbornness nor anything else about him. She wouldn't be around long enough. What was there about Belinda Diamond that made him forget who he was and who she was?

"If you were going to be here for any length of time, you might. But, of course, you'll be looking for a place of your own tomorrow, and we probably won't see each other again."

"I don't know so much about that." She reached over and squeezed his arm. "I don't like to let go of friends. Good friends are too hard to come by."

He felt as if he'd stepped into a pool of honey and was getting in deeper every minute. For a man who handled multimillion-dollar business deals on a regular basis, he was making a complete fool of himself with one sweet simple woman.

"Hmm," he said, neither agreeing nor disagreeing. Fortunately the dining room was just around the corner. "Well, here we are."

The familiarity of the setting grounded him in reality once more. Standing underneath his sparkling chandelier, pouring wine from his Waterford crystal decanter, he was completely in charge once more.

"Would you like a glass of wine?"

"Oh, Lordy me, no. The last time I had wine I got so wobbly I nearly fell off my high-heeled shoes. I didn't have all that much, either. Charlie said I must be allergic or something."

Laughing at herself, Belinda glided around the dining room, running her hand over the carved backs of chairs, stopping to admire the paintings on the walls, tilting her head sideways and back to look up at the chandelier.

Reeve didn't say anything immediately, but stood sipping his wine, watching her over the rim of his glass. With the lights sparkling down on her hair she looked like a long cool glass of lemonade. She was a tall woman, much taller than Sunny. With the right clothes and the right manners she would be elegant.

"Who is Charlie?" he asked. Not that it mattered, he told himself.

"Charlie Crocket. I met him at the Bull Pit up in St. Louis. He was wearing a cowboy hat about two sizes too big for his head, and he had the sweetest smile I've seen on a man. And Lordy, could he sweet-talk a woman."

Reeve was liking Charlie Crocket less every minute. He supposed there were lots of men who could sweet-talk the gullible Belinda Diamond. Knowing he would never stoop to such tactics made him feel noble.

"What is the Bull Pit?"

"A dance hall. I was a cocktail waitress. You should have seen my costume—a little old skirt that barely covered my privates and a fringed bra about as big as a handkerchief. Charlie said I looked like a ripe plum, fixing to pop off the tree."

Reeve nearly choked on his wine. "Indeed," he said when he had regained his composure. "And what else did Charlie say?"

"Lots. But I never let him pick my plums, I can tell you that."

"A woman of principle."

"You bet your boots."

Belinda lost interest in the subject and turned her inspection to the silver laid out in gleaming perfection on his table.

"Would you just look at that?" she said, lifting a fork. "It's like something a king would use. I never knew why anybody would want such fancy stuff to eat with. Me? I had some china that came from the grocery store. Got it with coupons. It was right nice. Had little blue chickens running around the border."

Reeve pictured Belinda dressed in her red high-heeled shoes and her sequined dress, sitting down to a modest meal served on cheap plates decorated with blue chickens. There was something comfortable and very homey about the picture. For a brief moment he felt nostalgic. He remembered a time when his own

life had been simple—before he'd started his business,
before he'd married Sunny Sinclair Wentworth.

He recalled his bachelor days, living in a two-room
apartment, putting together deals on a six-dollar por-
table phone he'd bought at a discount store. It all
seemed so long ago.

Belinda was inspecting the velvet draperies now,
running her hands up and down their soft folds. She
turned to him, smiling.

"One of these days I'm going to have me a house
of my own. I'm going to put lace curtains in the windows and geraniums on the front porch, and in the
evenings after work, I'm going to sit in a rocking chair
at the window and watch the rest of the world scur-
rying by doing all the things people get in a hurry
over. Me? I'll be listening to the birds sing through
the open window in the summertime, and in the winter
I'll listen to a little music on the radio."

Against his will, Reeve was caught up in her vision.
He could picture her in the rocking chair, feel her con-
tentment. In the space of one evening, he'd learned
more about Belinda Diamond than he knew about
most women after six months. Besides that, he found
himself *wanting* to know about her and interested in
her background, her philosophies, her tastes in food
and music.

With a start he realized that he was fascinated by
her. It was a kind of subtle fascination that had
sneaked up on him. And it was the dangerous variety,
fed not by awareness of her as a woman, but by in-

terest in her as a human being. He had neither time nor room for another person in his life.

He set his wineglass on a silver tray, then pulled out a chair for her. She looked at him with wise watchful eyes.

"You can sit here, Miss Diamond, on my right." *Miss Diamond, was it now?* Belinda took the seat he offered and wondered what she had done wrong. Lordy, the possibilities were so endless it was mindboggling. She'd never had dinner in such a fancy house. She'd never eaten off plates so delicate they looked like they would break if you put too many peas on them. What was more, she didn't know how she was supposed to eat with two forks. One had always been enough for her. And three spoons. What in the world did you do with three spoons?

"Thank you," she said as she slid into her seat. That was plain good manners, and she knew about manners. Her mother hadn't been a Southerner for nothing. "This certainly is a big table just for two," she added to fill the awkward silence between them.

"The children will be joining us."

"Oh."

The seconds slowly crawled by, each one scratching along Belinda's nerves. She fidgeted in her chair, wondering how women of means dealt with such moments as this, sitting in an elegant room with a handsome man. She guessed they'd talk about art or something. Well, she was no woman of means, but she had practically been born talking. She could talk to anybody about anything.

Suddenly she focused on the most dramatic piece of art in the room, the enormous portrait of a woman, hanging on the wall behind Reeve's chair. She had been dying to ask him about it from the minute she'd seen it, and she guessed now was the right time, what with the conversation lagging till it was about to stall.

"That's a beautiful woman. Is she somebody real?"

"Yes. She was my wife."

At last she had a conversation started. Gazing at the portrait, she continued her winning tack.

"She sure was beautiful."

"Many people said so."

"You know, her hair looks kind of like mine. I guess you noticed."

"I did."

He wasn't saying much, but at least he was talking. Belinda was grateful for that, though it did seem he ought to do a bit better. He was a man who could use a few lessons in the art of conversation.

"Just fancy that. I must have given you quite a turn coming up the street with hair like your dead wife's." There was a silence from Reeve's end of the table. Keeping her eyes pinned on the portrait as if it were a beacon of hope, Belinda rattled on. "Was she tall like me?" No answer. "For a minute there I'll bet you thought I was a ghost." Deadly silence. "That is, if you believed in ghosts."

The silence was so huge now that it roared in Belinda's ears. She looked at Reeve and almost flinched. The expression on his face was thunderous, almost murderous.

Well, for goodness' sake. She knew she wasn't the most brilliant conversationalist in the world, but she hadn't been that bad. She refused to back down from his stare.

"You are nothing like Sunny, Miss Diamond," he said at last. "In fact, you don't even remotely resemble her."

"Oh-h-h," she said, drawing out the syllable, her eyes and mouth as round as cherries. Her first impulse was to straighten him out about his manners. Land, he was as prickly as an old porcupine. He certainly could use a lesson or two in behaving himself. Then she remembered that she was a guest in his house, and where in the world would she go tonight if he threw her out?

In the end she folded her hands in her lap and lowered her eyes to shut out his face. From now on, she decided, she'd let him do the talking. That way, she'd be sure not to make any more mistakes.

She was saved further embarrassment by the children's entrance into the dining room. They were chattering and laughing, and Belinda had plenty to talk about with them. She remembered what it was like to be a child and interested in such things as building frog houses and making mud pies and playing hopscotch and skip-the-rope and trying to catch fireflies in the summertime.

The three of them soon had a lively conversation going that lasted all the way through the soup, though why in the world they had so many spoons just to eat soup with, Belinda couldn't have said. She was surprised when Quincy took the soup bowl and brought more food. Land, wouldn't it be easier to bring it all out at one time and get it over with? She'd never seen a meal take so long. She reckoned fancy folks spent half their time waiting for their food.

Though it was nice having the time to sit around the table and talk. She believed she was partaking of what was called a "leisure meal," sort of like the leisure suits that were so popular several years back. Charlie Crocket still had one that he was partial to. She wished Charlie could see her now. Wouldn't he bust a button?

"Did you really have a pet firefly?" Mark asked, bringing Belinda's attention back to the subject at hand.

"I sure did. Called him Wayne. I was living down in South Carolina at the time. Every evening I'd go out in the yard and say, 'Come on over here, Wayne. I want to talk to you.'"

"And did he come?" Betsy asked.

"Most times he would, but sometimes he was stubborn and wouldn't come until I promised to tell him a story."

Betsy clapped her hands. "Will you tell *us* a story?"

Belinda glanced at Reeve. It was practically the first

time she'd looked at him during the whole meal. His temper had improved a little. She guessed it was due to the roast beef. It was the best she'd ever had. Anyhow, his black eyes didn't look like they could cut you in half at twenty paces, and if she looked real close and used her imagination, she might even say he was trying to smile. She smiled back.

"Perhaps Miss Diamond will consider telling you a story after dinner, children. Dinnertime is for conversation, not stories."

A fat lot of conversation he'd thrown into the pot. Belinda took back her smile. It was wasted on him. What a shame. A man that handsome and with two beautiful kids and a big fancy house to boot ought to have a lot to smile about. She turned away from him and back to Betsy and Mark. Now there were two little people who knew how to make a body feel at home.

"How about if we sit down together on that big old couch I saw in your front parlor after dinner and I tell you *six* stories?"

"That's kind of you, Miss Diamond," Reeve said.

"Kindness is easy when you like somebody. I like Betsy and Mark. Quincy, too. She's nice."

Reeve noticed that his name was left off the roster of people she liked. Funny that such a silly thing should bother him. Of course, he had given her cause not to like him, overreacting as he had to that business about the portrait. If he could undo what he'd said and start all over, he would. But he supposed it was just as well that he was excluded from her list of nice people. It was best to keep a distance from this woman who already had him thinking that cheap stockings with rhinestone hearts looked good.

"I'm delighted you're so appreciative of my family."

"You don't look delighted," Belinda blurted, and then she clapped her hand over her mouth. Now she'd done it.

For a moment Reeve looked as if he had been told an earthquake was fixing to happen right under his chair and carry him off to Glory Land, and then he started to laugh. Belinda was so relieved she nearly said her prayer of thanks out loud.

"I suppose I have been somber. Quincy sometimes calls me a bear." Reeve inclined his head toward Belinda. "My apologies, Miss Diamond."

"Lordy, if you don't stop calling me Miss Diamond, I'm not ever going to forgive you for being an old sore-tailed bear."

"Belinda it is, then."

"Well, now. That's better. It makes me feel perky again with everybody smiling and happy." She picked up her fork and speared a piece of pecan pie. When it was halfway to her mouth, she paused to smile at Reeve. "Don't you think life is sometimes so grand that if it gets any better you'll just swoon?"

"I haven't given the quality of life much consideration lately."

"I guess a man like you gets so busy counting his money he can't take the time to swoon."

Reeve chuckled again. "You're probably right."

Quincy came in to whisk away the dessert plates.

"We'll have coffee in the den, Quincy," Reeve told her.

Belinda stood up. "I'll help you, Quincy."

"Thank you, honey, but I been bringin' Mr. Reeve his coffee since he was knee-high, and they's some things don't need changin'." Quincy waved her apron at them. "Now ya'll get on in the den and let old Quincy do her job. Scat now."

Reeve continued his study of his guest as he escorted her into the den. He had watched her all through the meal, silently marveling at the great pleasure she took in simple things. When she had talked about her childhood with Betsy and Mark, her face had lit up as if illuminated by a thousand fireflies. Her pleasure was genuine, too. Reeve had dealt with people long enough to know the difference between falseness and sincerity.

And now, entering his den, Belinda was oohing and ahhing and running her hands over his Chinese lacquered cabinets as if she had walked into the castle of one of her fairy tales. What was more, his children were enchanted with her. Her wonder infected them with high spirits, so that their laughter caroled through the house.

"Won't you sit down, Belinda? Quincy will be in shortly with the coffee." Reeve sat in a wing chair that afforded him a view of the entire room.

Belinda sat in the middle of the sofa, adjusting her

skirt and crossing her legs. Then she leaned down and smoothed her hands over her calves, as if checking to see if her stockings were in place. If the gesture had been calculated, Reeve would have been appalled. But it was totally artless—and so unexpectedly sensuous he felt the heat rise in his body. He wanted to tear his gaze away from her, but he couldn't. Her hair hung in a shining curtain down the side of her face as she bent over her leg.

Suddenly she parted her silken curtain of hair and glanced up at him through the folds of gold. "Are they straight now?"

"I beg your pardon?"

"My rhinestone hearts. Are they straight?"

"Um...yes."

"Good. When I'm all spiffed up, I like to stay that way, else what was the use of getting that way in the first place? Don't you agree?"

"Indeed." At the moment he would have agreed with anything she said, for his mind was still on that perfect row of hearts glittering down the side of her slim legs. He swung his attention to her hands. They were at rest now in her lap, but the way she had run them down her legs had been mesmerizing. In fact, she always used her hands in a sensuous manner. The way she touched his car, the way she touched his furniture, the way she reached up from time to time and smoothed her hair made him crazy inside. He must be going mad.

Reeve was saved when Quincy came in with the

coffee. Belinda added two spoons of sugar and lots of cream to hers. He should have guessed she'd like it that way.

"Betsy...Mark..." Belinda smiled at his children, curled on either side of her. "Are you ready for your stories now?"

"Yes," they said at the same time.

"Tell the bestest one first," Betsy added.

Quincy, who joined them for coffee, leaned forward in her chair, as fascinated as Reeve's children by the folksy tales Belinda was weaving. Reeve knew he should go. Betsy and Mark were well entertained, and Quincy would watchdog them until bedtime, when he was called upon to tuck them in. Mountains of work waited in his office, and he needed to catch up, for tomorrow he would be interviewing nannies. But he was under Belinda's spell. He couldn't make himself leave. Her stories were not mere tales to entertain his children, although he supposed that's how she perceived them; they were clues to the philosophy of the storyteller. The invincibility of the human spirit shone through all of them. They were stories of courage and bravery and the bright shining light of a spirit that could be neither daunted nor tamed.

Reeve was so caught up in Belinda and her stories that he didn't even note the passing of the hours. It was Quincy who finally announced it was way past the children's bedtime. They hugged Belinda and thanked her for the stories, then followed Quincy dutifully to their bedrooms.

Left alone with his guest, Reeve found himself still reluctant to part from her.

"You seem to have a way with children, Belinda."

"Lordy, I ought to. After Mother left I practically raised my two younger sisters. We never could afford a television set, so I had to do something to keep them occupied and out of trouble. You might say I learned to tell stories in self-defense."

Reeve refilled their coffee cups and watched as Belinda loaded hers with milk and sugar. She noticed him watching.

"I have a sweet tooth," she confessed. "I like sweet things so well it's a wonder I'm not big as a barrel. I guess I burn off all the calories by talking so much."

"Have you given any thought to what sort of work you will do here in Tupelo?"

"Oh, I can do just about anything—sew, cook, clean, type, cut hair. You might say I'm a jack-of-all-trades."

Any other woman in her position—homeless and probably almost penniless—would have been cringing with fear at her prospects, but Belinda remained unflappable. While he realized that her future was no concern of his, he didn't feel right just giving her a night's lodging, then letting her walk out his door tomorrow.

She had said she could type. Perhaps he could make room for her in his typing pool.

"You have business-school training?" he asked.

"No. Taught myself to type on Daddy's old upright.

The hunt-and-peck system, he called it. That was way back when we were living in Louisiana and he was having a whirl at being a newspaper man.''

"I see." Strike Belinda Diamond from his typing pool. Her hunt-and-peck system would give Gloria Grubbs a heart attack; and he'd have to hire a new senior business manager. He sipped his coffee, deep in thought.

"Well, now, look here..." Belinda set her coffee aside and crossed the room to stand in front of his chair. "You get that worried look right off your face. I sure don't want you thinking you have to try to find me a job, just because you were kind enough to let me stay the night in your house. Besides—" she paused, lifting her chin in a defiant gesture that set her hair a-swing. "—I've come to town a brand-new woman. I'm done with depending on somebody else. From now on I'm in charge of my own life."

Having finished her declaration of independence, she walked back to the sofa, her skirt dancing around her slim legs. It was a jaunty little walk that set his pulse racing. He glanced toward the double doors. Quincy had closed them behind her, as if she expected Reeve to need privacy with Belinda Diamond.

The doors were massive; the house was well built. A full-scale war could be conducted in each room with absolute assurance that the battle would not be heard in any other part of the house.

If Quincy could read his thoughts now, she would be delighted. Right now he was considering exactly how it would feel to hold Belinda Diamond's lithe body against his, to run his hands through her silky hair and down the length of her rhinestone-shimmering legs.

Thank God she had said she could take care of herself. Little did she know that she was saving him from himself. And now...the sooner he got out of his den with the closed door and the lamplight gleaming on Belinda's hair, the better off he would be.

"I applaud your independence, Belinda. If you will allow me, I'll drive you into town tomorrow, perhaps to the employment office."

"Shoot, if you can just plant my feet on Main Street, I can have me a job in no time flat. I don't mind work, and people find that out quick enough. I never have had any trouble finding me a job, no matter where I am."

"Agreed. Main Street it is." Reeve stood up, relieved that his evening with Belinda Diamond had drawn to a close. She stood, too, taking her cue from him.

"I'm going to tuck the children in, and then I have work to do here in my office. Please feel free to indulge yourself. I have a vast library, and the television is here...." He pulled aside the doors of an entertainment center to demonstrate. "There are even videotapes—mostly Walt Disney, I'm afraid—if you want to watch a movie. And, of course, I have quite a collection of music—jazz, classical, blues."

Belinda looked at the entertainment center with a certain longing in her eyes, then shrugged.

"Oh, well...I'm sort of tuckered out. It was a long

ride on the bus from Augusta, Georgia, all the way to Tupelo, Mississippi.''

"Of course." He escorted her from the den, then turned to her in the hallway. "I have some business to take care of here at home in the morning. If you don't mind waiting, I'll drive you into town after I have finished.''

"Thank you, Reeve." She offered her slim hand, and he held it a bit too long. Then he watched as she climbed the curving staircase to her bedroom.

He didn't know why he had thought she needed someone to teach her how to walk. There was a daredevil sort of elegance to her carriage, as if she were confident she was someone special. At the top of the stairs she turned slowly, smiling.

"Good night, Reeve."

"Good night, Belinda."

She lifted her slim hand until it was touching her lips, then ever so slowly, she blew him a kiss. The beauty of the gesture mesmerized him. He stood in the hallway gazing upward long after she had disappeared from the top of the stairs. And then he found himself touching his own face as if her kiss had actually landed there.

Don't be a fool, Reeve Lawrence.

His voice echoed in the empty hallway, and he became aware that he was talking to himself. He muttered a heartfelt oath, then quickly left the hallway where the presence of Belinda Diamond still lingered.

Chapter Three

Reeve had started his interviews at eight o'clock that morning and already he had eliminated five nannies. He was beginning to despair. He turned his full attention to the current candidate, Miss Caroline Upchurch. So far, she was doing well in the interview. She had the right background, the right education.

"How do you discipline children, Miss Upchurch?" he asked suddenly, treading into treacherous waters.

"I slap their faces."

"You slap their faces?"

"Mr. Lawrence, there's no need to roar. My hearing is perfectly sound."

"It's not your hearing I question, Miss Upchurch, it's your judgment. You may go."

"But you didn't even ask about my background in art."

"Miss Upchurch, under no circumstances would I entrust my children to the care of a woman who believes in physical violence—even if you had painted the Sistine Chapel." He stood up, dismissing her. "Goodbye, Miss Upchurch."

She sniffed as she walked haughtily toward his office door. When she opened it, he caught a glimpse of Belinda Diamond, his first of the morning. She was wearing denims and a bright red shirt, and she was apparently engaged with his children in some sort of game. Betsy and Mark's squeals of laughter echoed through his open door.

He followed Miss Upchurch and stood leaning in his doorway. His son and daughter were hopping on the marble squares in the hallway, and Belinda was cheering them on. They didn't see him at first, and he enjoyed watching them.

Suddenly Belinda turned. Her face lit in a huge smile at the sight of him. "Hi!" She waved, then motioned him over. "Come join us."

"What are you playing?" He left his place at the door to stand beside her. She smelled like roses.

"Hopscotch. Your hall is the perfect place. It already has squares laid out and everything. We didn't even have to draw them off with chalk."

"You have chalk?"

"Sure. Got it from Mark's room."

"And you were going to draw squares in the hall?"

She put her hands on her hips and squared her chin.

"It wipes right off. And anyhow, it's raining outside. The children can't play out in the rain."

"Hmm..." He considered her closely. She took his scrutiny in stride, looking him squarely in the eye. Belinda Diamond was not a woman who was easily intimidated.

Quite suddenly Reeve was overtaken with an idea so simple he wondered why he hadn't thought of it sooner.

"Would you mind stepping into my office?"

"Look, if it's about the chalk—"

"Forget the chalk—carry on, children. Belinda will be back soon." He was scrupulously careful not to touch her as he escorted her into his office. But even so, the fragrance of roses washed over his senses, reminding him of long walks in the moonlight on summer nights when the roses were in full bloom. He couldn't remember the last walk he'd had on a summer evening.

They stepped into his office, and he closed the door behind them. Belinda let out a big sigh. Thank goodness, he wasn't upset about the hopscotch game on his fancy marble floor. And whatever he wanted to talk to her about couldn't be all that bad, not in a room that looked as good as this one. It was homey and comfortable, not as elegant and forbidding as his dining room and his den. There were lots of books on the wall and window shades at the windows, drawn up so she could see the rain tapping against the panes. His desk chair looked cozy and big enough for two.

She slid a sideways glance at Reeve. My, he was wonderfully made. What would it be like to have a man like that all to yourself in a room like this? The first thing she would do was cuddle up to his broad chest in that big old desk chair. The thought made her smile.

"Won't you sit down, Belinda?"

She was still smiling when she sat down, even though Reeve had taken the chair behind his desk and now seemed more remote, like a king sitting on his throne.

She folded her hands in her lap and waited quietly for him to speak, but he acted as if he'd forgotten why he'd wanted her in here. He was as still as Abraham Lincoln in his great big old stone chair in Washington, D.C.—and nearly as scary-looking. Lord, she wished he'd smile. With his eyes all dark and his face so solemn, Reeve looked like he might be sizing her up for his dinner.

Belinda had never been the nervous type, so she didn't fidget. Instead she looked him right in the eye.

Finally Reeve spoke. His voice was large as it shattered the silence. "I have had a bit of ill luck this morning. I've been interviewing nannies. Unsuccessfully, I might add."

"That bunch of women I've seen parading in and out of here?"

"Yes."

Her face split into a big smile. "I don't blame you

for calling them nannies. Especially that last one. She really did look like a goat.''

Reeve burst into laughter. "Point well made." He sobered and picked up his letter opener. It was cool and heavy, and it gave him something to do with his hands—though he had never had trouble with his hands until he'd met Belinda Diamond.

"You see," he began again, "since my wife's death, I have employed a succession of women to look after my children."

"I see." Belinda's heart went flip-flopping around her chest, and she felt as if all the air had been sucked out of the room. But she didn't dare get her hopes up too high. She knew the meaning of disappointment.

"Tomorrow I must leave for a business trip to San Francisco, and I would like to have someone here to help Quincy with the children. She's getting too old to manage the household and the children, too."

Belinda didn't know why he was beating around the bush so. He was beginning to make her nervous. She wanted to blurt out to him that he say what was on his mind and get her off needles and pins. But she didn't. A part of being a new woman was learning not to speak before she thought. So she sat very still and looked at him steadily so he would see she was a woman who could take care of herself under any circumstances.

His face had softened a little, and when he spoke, so had his voice. "My children like you, Belinda."

"I like them."

"They are very precious to me."

"All children are precious."

Reeve relaxed a little. He wasn't given to impulse, and yet he had acted on impulse by bringing Belinda Diamond into his office and hinting that he might have a job for her. Now it seemed the best way to approach the interview was not to conduct an interview at all, but to continue with this informal discussion. Belinda was the kind of artless truthful woman who held nothing back. He had already learned enough about her to suspect that she would be a good nanny—temporarily, of course. And now, the things she said confirmed his opinion.

He plowed full speed ahead. "Betsy and Mark can sometimes be naughty and full of pranks."

"Shoot, you should have seen all the things I got into when I was their age. My daddy swore I was going to give him a heart attack before he reached thirty."

"I suppose you took your whippings."

"Whippings!" Her eyes got darker as she leaned forward in her chair. "My daddy never laid a hand on me. And I'll tell you another thing—anybody who does that to a child is a yellow-bellied, lily-livered coward who deserves to be strung up so the buzzards can gnaw on his insides."

Reeve's big laugh pealed around the room. Belinda had certainly spared no words in telling him what he wanted to know.

"Well, I didn't think it was all that funny." Belinda

stood up. "And if you're the kind of man who whips his children, then I'm in the wrong house. I don't even want to ride in the car with you down to Main Street, thank you very much."

Head high, she began her regal exit. Reeve hurried around his desk and caught her by the shoulders. Slowly he turned her back around. She tilted her head to look up at him, her eyes still blazing.

"I would never touch my children in anger, nor would I allow anyone else to punish them in such a manner. I was merely testing you, Belinda."

"Why didn't you just come right out and ask? I'd have told you the truth."

"I know that."

Her face was still tilted up to his, and she was so close he could feel the pleasant warmth of her body and smell the intoxicating fragrance of roses. He had held on to her too long. What was more, he didn't want to let go. The knowledge was so disturbing that he put her away from him almost roughly and hurried back to his chair. When he was safely behind his desk, he braced his hands and said softly, "Please don't go, Belinda."

"Well, I swear..." The legs of her jeans rubbing together made a soft swishing sound as she walked back to her chair. The sound crawled along Reeve's nerves, with little cat's feet. He felt as if every part of his body had burst suddenly to life. Then Belinda sat down and the sensual sound of her movements stopped. "What some men won't do to get a rise out of woman."

She fanned her hot face with her hand. Even that movement was elegant and somehow sexy. Reeve admonished himself to get under control.

"I have a business proposition for you, Belinda," he said, very much in charge once more.

"I'm all ears."

"Tomorrow, I leave on a trip to San Francisco, and I'd like to hire you as temporary nanny for my children."

"Temporary?"

The disappointment was clearly written on her face. So be it, he thought. He wasn't about to make any long-term commitments to a woman whose mere presence was enough to shake both his judgment and his reserve. Besides, she was not suitable for the long haul. Betsy and Mark needed a woman well versed in art and literature and music, someone who could give them the training that Sunny would have if she were alive.

"Since you're planning to settle in Tupelo, I know you're looking for a job with more future, Belinda. And I certainly don't want to stand in your way."

"Shoot, you're not in my way. I guess I'd just go around you if you got in the way."

"So—" he leaned back in his chair "—are you willing to work for me for the next few days, Belinda?"

She would have crawled on her hands and knees

and slobbered all over his feet for the chance to stay in his fairy-tale castle a while longer. Just think of all the grand times she would have exploring! On the other hand, she didn't want to appear too anxious. If you got too anxious, employers cut the pay down until it was next to nothing.

Belinda decided to speak right out, as bold as you please.

"How much does it pay?"

He named a figure that had her gasping in surprise it was so high. "Lord have mercy! That sounds like so much money it's almost wasteful!"

"Good. Then it's agreed. I'll have Quincy inform you about the children's routine, then you may consider your duties officially begun." He stood up, and waited for her to understand that the interview was over and she was being dismissed.

Instead, she snuggled down in her chair and gave his office a lively inspection. "Just think—me in this wonderful house for a few days." She smiled at him. "Won't that be just grand?"

"I...suppose so." He hovered behind his desk like a benevolent professor indulging a favorite student.

"Last night when I was bundled up under that big soft comforter of yours in that pretty bedroom, I pretended this was my house. That every bit of this was all mine." She waved her hand around the room to encompass his bookshelves and his desk and his works of art and his Persian rug. "Why, I was just as happy as if I had died and gone to the Glory Land. That's how wonderful I think this house is.''

He sank back into his chair. There was nothing alarming about Belinda's vision. In fact, he found it to be rather flattering. He had always taken pride in his home, and it pleased him to see that she loved it so.

"I'm glad you like it.''

"Like it! Mercy me.'' She came out of her chair, as graceful and quick as a gazelle, and moved around till she was standing beside his chair. Her heavenly scent wafted over him, and her nearness set his pulse racing.

She reached out and ran her hand lovingly along the back of his chair. He could barely feel her touch on the back of his neck. Strange stirrings brought his body to full alert. He reached for his letter opener, gripping it hard.

"If I lived in this big old house permanent-like...'' She paused, gazing down at him. Her voice and her eyes had both gone dreamy. "You know, maybe with a husband and two kids all my own...'' Her hand played softly along the back of his chair again, making his blood race. "Why, I 'spect I might have a hard time getting all my work done. Take this chair, for instance. If I had a husband, why, I'd curl up in his lap in this big old comfortable chair and smooch to my heart's content.'' Her hands whispered along the leather again. "Smooching's nice, don't you think?''

"Hmm...'' He cleared his throat. "I suppose...''

The scent of roses heightened his senses, and her warm hand slid along the back of his chair once more, grazing his neck. Suddenly his body responded like an old soldier who had been out of battle too long but who'd never forgotten how to win the war.

Blindly he reached for the intercom. *"Quincy!"* He knew he was bellowing, but he was past caring. *"Will you come into my office?"*

Belinda jumped back from his chair as if she'd been shot. Land, she'd done it now. All that money down the tube just because she got carried away over his desk chair. Well, it was more than that, really, she thought as she made her way back to her own chair. Actually, she got carried away by him—by Reeve Lawrence. There was something powerful about that man. He was like a magnet drawing things toward him. Her, for one. She had felt the pull, and she had just naturally followed it. That's how she had ended up behind his chair, running her hands along the back, for goodness' sake.

And now she was going to pay the consequences. He was going to fire her even before she got started. Worse yet, he was going to have Quincy show her the door.

She licked her lips. Maybe if she apologized—*"Belinda,"* he shouted before she could even open her mouth. She jumped again. He was making her as nervous as a cat, and she'd never even quivered at horror movies.

"About that chair now," she said. "I'm sorry."

God, it was bad enough to be in the state he was in, without her reminding him of the way her hands had slid gently along the back of his chair, brushing his neck like a cool summer breeze. He tried to rein himself in. The first thing he did was moderate his voice.

"Quincy is going to take you into the children's quarters and explain how I like things done." Belinda looked at him with eyes as big as pansies, and her pink tongue licked her lips again. He wished she wouldn't do that. It was driving him mad.

Quincy's coming through the door saved him.

"You yelled, Mr. Reeve?"

"Sorry, Quincy. Please come in."

"That's more like it." Quincy came into the room, bringing with her the smell of cinnamon. "With you yellin' around here, comin' out of that box on the wall like a cyclone, I plumb tore the head off a gingerbread boy." She rubbed her hands on her apron. "You need to settle down a little. Take life a little easier 'fore you kill yourself with a stroke."

He was already settling down some, thanks to her familiar and comforting presence. With Quincy in the room, life seemed normal again. Belinda Diamond was just a stranger passing through, and he was once more a businessman hiring a nanny.

"Quincy, I've hired Belinda as temporary nanny."

"Saints be praised." Quincy folded her hands in a prayerful attitude and lifted her eyes to heaven.

Reeve ignored her antics. "Will you please escort

her to the children's quarters and familiarize her with their routine?''

"Why don't you do it yourself? I got gingerbread boys burnin'.''

He would never have tolerated such impertinence in anyone else. But in the Lawrence household, Quincy reigned supreme. "I'm willing to sacrifice gingerbread boys.'' He stood up, now that he could. "I'm going to my office downtown, Quincy. I'll be back late this evening in time to tuck the children into bed.'' He left the room quickly.

"What about lunch?'' Quincy called after him.

"I'll grab a bite on the way to the office.''

He didn't even stop and turn around, but called over his shoulder, "Don't keep dinner for me, either. I'll order Chinese.''

The walk down his hall seemed endless. Fortunately his children weren't around to hamper his progress. He didn't want anything to stop his flight from Belinda Diamond, not even his beloved Betsy and Mark. At last his front door came into view. He felt as if he were a dying man lost in the desert, suddenly in sight of an oasis.

He burst through the door and headed blindly for his car. It wasn't until he was behind the wheel that he realized he had forgotten his briefcase. That couldn't matter, not now, not when getting out of that house was of paramount importance. He'd send his office manager back for it. Let them all think what they would.

The sound of his engine roaring to life was reassuring. He was a busy man, driving a powerful car to a powerful job. He was Reeve Lawrence, a man in charge of his world.

Belinda followed Quincy to the children's quarters, but her mind was still on her new boss. He'd said he would order Chinese food. Suddenly the big old house yawned empty, all the furniture rattling around like noisy ghosts. That was ridiculous, of course. Quincy and Betsy and Mark were there. But with Reeve gone...

"Now this is the children's bathroom," Quincy was saying. "They bathe every night at seven whether they's dirty or not. Mr. Reeve don't tolerate no changin' the schedule."

Belinda tried to concentrate, but her mind was still on Reeve. Funny how a house seemed different with somebody special inside. A hot flush came into her cheeks. Lord have mercy. Somebody special! Here she was already making a fool of herself over that man—after telling herself she wouldn't do any such thing.

"And, of course, they usually eat meals just as regular as a clock—breakfast at seven, lunch at twelve and dinner at eight, with a snack at four in the afternoon."

"But what if they're right in the middle of a game at four o'clock? Or what if they get hungry at three?"

"They ain't no changin' that neither. But I'll tell you a little secret. I got a cookie jar stashed in the kitchen that nobody but me and them kids knows about. Anytime they gets hungry, all they got to do is sneak by and dig in, and I acts like I'm not even lookin'."

Belinda and Quincy laughed together. Both of them were already liking the new arrangement enormously.

Belinda stayed busy the rest of the day, and it wasn't until nightfall that she had time to notice Reeve's continued absence. He was still at the office, she guessed, eating his lonely meal of Chinese food. She pictured him in another desk chair big enough for cuddling. My, my. If such a man belonged to her she'd be down at that office in a shake, perched on the edge of his desk with her shoes off and her stocking feet in his lap, laughing at something funny that had happened that day and eating bites of Chinese food off the same fork. Wouldn't that be just dandy?

She stood at the window of her bedroom, gazing out. The moon slithered from behind the trees, big as a yellow balloon.

"Belinda Stubaker," she whispered fiercely, "don't you dare go messing up this job on account of feeling swoony and foolish over the boss."

She stayed at the window a while longer, hoping for a glimpse of his car as he came up the driveway, but it got late and he never came. Quincy had said he always tucked the children into bed when he was in town. She guessed she'd run him off from his own children with all her talk of smooching in a big old desk chair.

It was bad enough that she was acting under an assumed name. The least she could do was learn to hold her tongue.

Sighing, she pressed her forehead against the windowpane. What did it hurt to watch out the window a while longer? A girl could dream, couldn't she?

Chapter Four

Reeve got up the next morning before anybody in the house was stirring. He went quietly down the stairs, carrying his suitcase and telling himself how much he liked early-morning solitude. Nobody around to muddle his thinking. Nobody around to clutter the tidiness of his house. Nobody around to distract him.

He liked it like that. Yessir. That's what he kept telling himself.

Downstairs he tiptoed into his children's bedrooms and kissed their sleeping faces. Always when he flew out before they awakened, he left chocolate kisses on their pillows. In each bedroom, he pulled the kisses out of his pockets and placed them gently on Mark's and then Betsy's pillows. Then he went outside and got into his car.

He sat behind the wheel, letting the engine warm

up and gazed back at his house. Something drew his attention upward. There was a face at the window, a lovely face surrounded by bright shiny hair. Belinda Diamond. The engine idled while he continued to stare at the face in the upstairs window.

Suddenly the window flew open, and her delicate hand fluttered toward her bow-shaped lips. Like a small bird, her hand floated gracefully downward, dropping the kiss in the direction of his car. Unconsciously he caught the kiss and pressed it against his own lips.

The engine idled louder, catching Reeve's attention. He went rigid with fury at himself. What was he doing? Had he lost his senses?

He tore out of the driveway as if the hounds of hell were barking at his heels. Belinda was still at the window. He didn't have to look back to know; he could *feel* her there, watching him with her big dark eyes, waving that lovely expressive hand.

He touched his lips again. Her kiss seemed to burn there.

An image of Sunny floated up before him—Sunny with her bright hair and her bright laughter, Sunny with her charm and her laughing eyes. She had always seen him off. She used to walk down the staircase with him, arm in arm. At the doorway she would stand on tiptoe and kiss him goodbye. It was a ritual he'd cherished.

"Sunny," he said, not knowing he had spoken aloud.

Her image began to fade, and in its place came the face of Belinda with her impertinent mouth and her mysterious eyes, Belinda with her rhinestoned stockings and her red spike-heeled shoes. She was outrageous and unconventional, a woman whose education had been on the back roads and in the beer joints and the cheap rooming houses of the world. And yet... twice she had blown him kisses in a manner as eloquent as any finishing-school lady, kisses he foolishly coveted and secretly longed for.

What was happening to him? It was a damned good thing he was going to San Francisco. As soon as he got back, he would drive Belinda Diamond to downtown Tupelo and let her out on Main Street, just as he had promised. With the money he was planning to pay her, she would be set for a long time, certainly long enough to find a decent job.

And then she wouldn't be his concern anymore. Once again she would be a stranger to him, and his life would go on as it had before she came, its carefully structured schedules hiding whatever flaws there were in the fabric of his daily routine.

After he had checked into his hotel in San Francisco, the first thing he did was call home. It was a part of his routine. The children needed to hear his voice and he needed to hear theirs. It would be midafternoon back home, almost time for their snack.

He dialed his home number and waited.

"Hello, there. I mean, Lawrence residence."

Reeve's hand tightened on the receiver. Belinda had answered the phone. Her voice brought her into his room as plainly as if she had made the trip to San Francisco with him.

"Where's Quincy?" He knew he was being rude, but he excused himself by claiming flight fatigue. His lack of manners had nothing whatsoever to do with the fact that he had hoped a thousand miles would take Belinda Diamond out of his life, at least temporarily.

"She's a dragon."

"She's a what?"

"Well, you see, it started raining along about noon, and I decided to build a castle in the den. So we set up the card table and draped it with a sheet, and Betsy decided the castle needed a dragon, and since I was the queen and she was the princess and Mark was the dashing knight in shining armor, Quincy had to be the dragon."

"That explains it, of course." Reeve couldn't disguise the indulgent tone of his voice. When Belinda told a story, she had a way of involving the listener, so that right now, standing in the middle of his generic hotel room with its standard puffy comforter on the bed and its ubiquitous white towels hanging on the bar in the bathroom and its strip of paper certifying that the toilet was sanitary, he was caught up in Belinda's make-believe castle.

The fantasy made him homesick. He couldn't remember the last time he'd been homesick.

"Quincy's down on the floor now, growling. Do you hear her?"

Belinda must have held the receiver out toward the castle, for Reeve caught the sounds of laughter and a deeper, more guttural sound that must have been Quincy's dragon.

"Did you hear her?" Belinda sounded breathless and cheerful. He wondered if she was wearing stockings with rhinestone hearts on the sides.

"She sounded right fierce to me."

Belinda's laughter pealed through the receiver, the happy sound filling his drab hotel room, making it seem less lonely. "I'll tell her you said that."

"Please do. Tell her if she keeps on making such a good dragon, I might have to increase her salary."

Reeve was feeling more cheerful himself. He hadn't engaged in frivolous small talk in years. He and Belinda laughed together, their voices mingling like singers harmonizing for a duet at a church social.

"My, my, it's just grand to hear your voice," Belinda said.

That sobered Reeve quickly enough. It would be best not to foster any false hopes she might have. "May I speak with my children, please?"

"Oh..." Her voice was colored with disappointment. There was a brief pause, and then her voice came back to him as perky as ever. "Well, naturally that's why you called. I knew that all along.... Mark!" she called, then another pause. "He's coming. He just had to park his horse. Oh, wait till you hear about the moat we're planning to build around the castle. It was all Mark's idea. We're going to… Wait a minute. Here's Mark.''

His son came on the line and Belinda Diamond was gone. Suddenly the emptiness of his hotel room struck Reeve, and a great lonesomeness settled in the pit of his stomach.

Reeve spent the next ten minutes listening to his children's happy chatter, and it wasn't until he had hung up the phone that he remembered he had never found out about the moat. He could just picture it: Belinda digging a trench in his Persian rug, and his children dumping in buckets of water. Quincy, of course, would be standing by with the mop, laughing her head off. She had always encouraged rowdiness in his children.

Reeve smiled. What did a Persian carpet matter? Happy children were the most important thing. And from the sounds of things, they were certainly happy with their new temporary nanny.

Reeve called home again that evening. He didn't usually make two calls home in the same day, but he figured these were unusual circumstances. After all, Belinda was new to the job, and he would be foolish not to make sure that her first day without him around had gone smoothly.

When she answered the phone, he smiled. He went on smiling as long as she kept saying into the receiver, ''Hello? Hello? Is anybody there?''

"It's Reeve."

"Reeve." She sort of sighed his name. Her voice sounded like a light breeze dancing through autumn leaves.

"I just called to…" His mind drifted off again. *To hear your voice,* he thought. *To make myself smile. To feel your presence in this lonesome hotel room.*

"Yes?"

"…to see how the children are."

"They're wonderful, of course. All bathed and fed and tucked into their beds, right on schedule. Well, almost. We were a little late with the baths on account of Mark's moat getting out of hand." She paused for breath, and Reeve hung on to the receiver, waiting for the sound of her voice. "See, we got kind of carried away cutting up all that blue paper for the water, and then Betsy decided it was hot in the castle under the table, and Quincy brought an oscillating fan out of her room, and the paper started blowing everywhere…. I'm afraid some of it might still be lurking around in the top bookshelves."

Reeve had a wonderful time imagining the four of them chasing after the paper moat. They would have been laughing like crazy. He wished he'd been there.

"You're awfully quiet, Reeve. Does this mean I'm fired?"

"Absolutely not."

"Are you having trouble on your end of the phone?"

"No. Why?"

"Because all of a sudden you seem to be roaring."

Of course he had been roaring. Just the thought of firing Belinda Diamond was enough to make him bellow like a bull. How anybody could be heartless enough to fire the woman was beyond him.

"You'll have to excuse me, Belinda. I must have had a frog in my throat." He cleared his throat for effect. It was clearly time to end this conversation. "Keep up the good work, Belinda."

"Will you call again?"

There was a long silence. Then Reeve said, "Yes, I'll call again." Another silence in which the sound of their breathing mingled over the long-distance line. "I'll call every day—to check on the children."

"Oh. Well, goodbye. Sweet dreams, Reeve."

He spent so long thinking about "sweet dreams" that she had hung up the phone before he could say goodbye. It was just as well. Things were getting out of hand in San Francisco as surely as they had in Tupelo.

Maybe it was his age. Maybe forty was too old to cope with bringing up two children and dealing with a succession of nannies.

He stretched himself across his bed and stared up at the ceiling. Wouldn't it be nice if everything back home were settled into such a perfect routine that he didn't have the constant worry of keeping everything in control with his bare hands and the force of his iron will?

* * *

The next morning when Reeve awoke, the first thing he thought of was calling home. He picked up his watch and looked at the luminous dial. It was a good time to call, but he decided to wait a few hours.

Right before his luncheon meeting he slipped upstairs to his room and dialed home. Quincy answered, and disappointment washed over him.

"Mr. Reeve! You ought to see them children. Happy as pigs in the sunshine. That Belinda Diamond is somethin' else, I tell you. Hmm-mm."

She said all that before he even had a chance to do more than identify himself.

"Quincy," he said, "Quincy—"

But she rattled on. "Miss Belinda's been showin' them children how to cook." Her booming laughter sounded over the line. "You ought to see this kitchen. Looks like a cyclone done hit it. Chocolate everywhere." She laughed again. "Them children ain't had this much fun in a month of Sundays."

"May I speak to them?" Reeve asked when Quincy paused for breath.

"They's all up in the tree. Let me see which one is closest to the ground."

Reeve heard her heavy footfalls, then the sound of her voice yelling, "Miss Belinda! Telephone!"

Quincy got back on the line. "She's a-comin'. Now don't you worry 'bout a thing. Just go on and have a high ol' time out there. Me and Miss Belinda is gettin' on just like a house on fire. And...well, I done told you about them children...Here's Miss Belinda."

Funny how the sound of a voice could put a shine on the entire day. Reeve found himself smiling from the minute Belinda said her first lilting hello.

"Hello? Hello? I'm so out of breath. Can you hear me, Reeve?"

"I hear you."

"We've been climbing a tree."

"Yes, I know."

"It was Mark's idea. That son of yours is quite lively."

"I suppose you climbed the tree, too?"

"Well, naturally. You don't think I'd let your children try something before I did. I had to check and see if all the limbs were sturdy enough."

"And were they?"

"Well, I got down in one piece except for a little scratch on my arm."

"Did you hurt yourself?"

"Shoot, no. Betsy kissed it and made it better."

"I see." Reeve imagined kissing Belinda's arm to make it better. He could almost smell the roses on her skin. His breathing got shallow, and he forgot what he'd been going to say next.

Fortunately Belinda didn't notice his silence. She talked on, as cheerful as a salesman in a car commercial, and all he had to do was listen to her stories and the musical sound of her voice.

The four days he was in San Francisco, calling home twice a day got to be a habit. And it was funny how often he hoped Belinda would be the one who answered the phone. As Quincy would say, "That just goes to show..." He didn't try to figure out what it went to show; he just drifted along, enjoying knowing that Belinda was making his children happy and that she was happy herself, and counting the days till he would be home.

Belinda was the first to see his car coming up the drive. "Reeve's home!" she yelled, and went racing through the front door and down the porch steps.

When he stepped out of the car, so handsome with the late-afternoon sun shining in his hair, she came to a screeching halt. Dear Lord in heaven, what was she thinking of? Fixing to jump into her boss's arms like he was Charlie Crocket come home on payday with a bonus in his pocket? Even Charlie hadn't much liked her habit of jumping all over him with big hugs and kisses. She could just imagine what Reeve Lawrence would do. Why, he'd disappear into himself like an oyster, leaving nothing but the hard shell for her to deal with.

She stopped beside the gardenia bush, put her hands behind her back and tried to look proper as befitted her station. Thank goodness he couldn't know that her skin was all a-tingle and her heart was pumping and her body felt warm and glowy, like she had been sitting in front of a good hot fire.

"Hello, Belinda," he said the minute he was out of

the car. That was all he said, just "hello," then stood there looking at her.

Belinda Stubaker, she warned herself, *just you remember he's your boss.*

"Reeve, it's good to have you home." She was proud of herself for sounding so calm and ladylike.

"It's good to be home."

He walked toward her and caught her elbow, and she shivered inside like dynamite had been set off next to her heart. He had been gone so long she had forgotten what being next to a powerful man felt like.

She managed to contain herself till they got inside the house, and then she was rescued by Mark and Betsy. While they hugged and kissed their daddy, Belinda sidled off and sank into a chair where she pressed her knees together and folded her hands tightly over her stomach. She thought she was going to be sick. Now, wouldn't that be embarrassing?

Any other person would be jumping for joy at the return of a boss who was fixing to pay you a lot of money. And she had at first. Jumped for joy, that is. But not necessarily because of her salary. Now all she could think about was that in the next twenty minutes or so, Reeve would pay her off and load her bag into his fancy car and drop her off somewhere on Main Street. She hoped she could act happy about the whole thing.

Mark and Betsy were both talking at once, and every now and then she could tell Reeve was adding his two cents' worth just by the rumble of that rich voice, but she didn't have any idea what they were saying. She was too busy trying to figure out how to act grateful when her heart was fixing to break in two.

"Belinda." She jumped at the sound of her name. Lordy, she was getting fidgety. Reeve walked to her chair and stood over her like some great god of the mountain. She could hardly get her breath. "Will you come with me to my office, please?"

She opened her eyes wide and noticed that Quincy was disappearing down the long marble hallway with Betsy and Mark. She wanted to call after them to stop, come back. As long as they were in the hall, she would be spared going into that office for her walking papers.

"Certainly," she said, sounding far more sophisticated than she had any right to sound. Maybe being in such a fancy house was rubbing off on her. Her daddy had always said she was a quick study and a great mimic. Why, back when she and her sisters went to the Saturday matinees at the old Strand Theater, where they showed all the classic movies, she could come back talking just like Bette Davis or Joan Crawford or Betty Grable and all those highfalutin stars.

In his office, Reeve motioned her to the same chair she had sat in the last time. Then he got behind his important-looking desk and sat in his chair, big enough for two. There was no mistaking his intent. Clearly he was the boss and she was the hired help, even if he did insist on calling her a nanny.

He propped his elbows on his desk, made a steeple with his fingers and seemed to be studying his hands to see if he had done it right. It was a long time before he spoke.

Belinda waited. She knew about being patient. Hadn't she spent many hours of her childhood waiting in her daddy's car in one strange town or another while he walked the streets looking for a job?

"Quincy and the children have made quite a case for you," Reeve said finally.

"I didn't know I was on trial."

Reeve laughed. Belinda thought that was a good sign.

"You know...this job was only temporary."

"I know. My suitcase is all packed and ready."

Reeve spent another long while in the study of his steepled hands. Thin lines etched themselves around his mouth.

"You are anxious to go, I suppose, anxious to get on with your life."

"Oh, no." She almost came out of her chair. He looked startled, and she sat back down and crossed her legs at the ankles like a lady. She had her pride. "Of course, I have my own life to live and all, but one of the best times I've ever had has been staying in this house these past few days, taking care of your children. They're wonderful. And so is Quincy. We've had us a ball while you've been gone."

"So I gathered."

They held each other in silent regard for a long time. A soft twilight began to gather outside the windows, and summer breezes sprang to life in the trees.

Reeve's checkbook was only four inches from his hand, but he felt a strange reluctance to reach for it. What was happening to him? Business had always been the easiest part of his life. Why was he hesitating about taking care of business with Belinda Diamond?

He looked down at his hands, still tightly entwined in a steeple. A little while longer, he said to himself. He would indulge his foolish need to keep her in his office a little while longer.

"It's almost dark outside," he said.

"I know."

"I believe our original bargain was that I would drive you to Main Street and leave you."

"That's what we said."

"Naturally I can't leave you on Main Street in the dark."

"You can take me to a motel."

Was she that eager to leave him? Was he such a bear that she couldn't wait to be out of his sight? She had said the past few days were one of the best times of her life, but that had nothing to do with him. She had specifically mentioned his house and his children.

Had he been fantasizing out in San Francisco? Had he imagined the magic that happened every time he called home and heard her voice? Men under pressure had done worse things.

His hand shot out and grabbed his checkbook. There was no need to prolong this parting. He wrote her check with a sure firm hand and slid it to her across the desk.

"I hope this proves satisfactory."

She read the amount, then quietly folded it and tucked it into her skirt pocket.

"Quite. Thank you," she said, then stood up.

She was ending their meeting. Reeve had to admire her style. He pushed back his chair and came around the desk. It was one of the few times in his life he was at a loss for words.

Belinda gazed steadily at him, her dark eyes luminous. "I'll get my suitcase." She moved toward the door.

"Wait."

She turned slowly around and stood watching him. He shoved his hands into pockets to keep from reaching for her.

"There's no need for you to leave tonight."

"You've paid me. My work here is finished."

"Would you allow me a small gesture of thanks? Will you spend one more night under my roof?"

Belinda didn't believe in long goodbyes. They hurt too much. Best to pack up and get out while the going was good, so to speak. But the remote look was gone from Reeve's face, and there was something in him that seemed to be crying out to her. She knew, though, that she didn't need to start off her new life by mixing herself up with somebody who needed as much fixing as Reeve Lawrence.

Still...he was giving her a chance to dream just a little while longer. Oh, she did love his house so!

"Yes. Thank you," she finally said. Lights seemed

to leap up in the center of his eyes, and she knew she couldn't spend the evening in his company, knowing that tomorrow they would part. "But if you don't mind, I'm a little tired. I think I'll spend the evening in my room. I'll say goodbye to Betsy and Mark, then grab a bite in the kitchen before I go upstairs."

"As you wish."

She left the room, and Reeve stood a long time watching the closed door. He didn't know what he was expecting. Perhaps that Belinda would come back into the room, laughing and talking about life being grand, running her hands over the back of his chair and sending his pulse racing. She had claimed to be tired. How could that be? Once she had told him life was too exciting to get tired and miss any of it.

The minutes ticked by and still the door to his office stayed closed. In his soundproof house, there was not even the murmur of voices to tell him he was not alone. He might have been the only person on the planet.

Suddenly he turned and slammed his palm down on his desk. The quick jolt of pain brought him back to his senses.

"Don't be a fool," he muttered, then strode from his office to spend some time with his children.

That night Reeve's dreams were haunted by a pair of bow-shaped lips and a sassy pair of legs clad in black silk stockings decorated with rhinestone hearts. Belinda Diamond was running down the staircase to meet him, her arms outstretched. Then the staircase dissolved and she was in a flaming sports car, plunging to the bottom of a ravine.

Reeve awoke in a sweat. He threw the covers back and walked to his bedroom window. There was a faint tinge of pink in the east. Soon it would be morning. He stood at his window, thinking, until the sun cleared the horizon and a new day was born. Then he dressed quickly and went downstairs.

He didn't see Belinda at first. She was sitting in a chair drawn close to the staircase, her face in shadow. His shoes clicked on the marble tile as he passed her.

"Good morning, Reeve."

At the sound of her voice, he whirled around. She was sitting with her feet together and her hands folded on her lap. A spray of artificial flowers decorated her left shoulder, and her cardboard suitcase sat at her feet. Even from the short distance that separated them, she looked small and faraway, as if she had already left his house and was rapidly disappearing from sight.

"I see you're packed and ready to go."

"Yes."

His footsteps sounded loud as he strode toward her. When he was even with her chair, he stopped.

"Belinda, I don't want you to go," he said simply.

She tipped her face up to him and gave him that steady head-on look he so admired.

"And what would I be doing if I stayed? My temporary job is over." She rose majestically, standing tall in her red spike-heeled shoes. "I don't plan to loll around this fancy house taking your charity."

Reeve laughed with the pleasure of her refreshing company and the beautiful simplicity of the plan that had come to him in the wee hours of the morning. She looked at him as if he had suddenly gone crazy, and he supposed he had. Or maybe he was just coming to his senses.

"Come with me," he said, taking her arm and hauling her unceremoniously down the hall to his office. He left her cardboard suitcase sitting in the hall.

"Where are you taking me?"

"I don't conduct business standing in the hallway."

"Business?"

He looked down at her, smiling. Why he hadn't seen the obvious sooner was beyond him. The thing he had been searching for was right under his nose. Forget a nanny well versed in the arts; what he needed was a reliable kindhearted nanny with common sense. "Yes, business. Miss Belinda Diamond, we're going to draw up your contract as my permanent nanny."

He was so pleased with himself that he didn't notice his slip of the tongue; but Belinda did. In amongst her visions of living in her dream house for the next ten years or so and having her very own room and lots of security and maybe a chance to put geraniums on the front porch, even if it wasn't really her porch, came a vision of herself as *Reeve's* nanny. Now there was a thought.

She turned her head sideways and grinned at him.

"I accept the job." In between caring for the children and helping Quincy, she would have plenty of time left over to work on Reeve Lawrence.

The first thing she thought she'd fix was his social life. All he ever did was work. It was high time the man started having a little fun.

Chapter Five

The sound of music came from Reeve's den, a strange haunting sort of music.

Belinda had been with him two weeks now, and his house seemed to be filled with the sounds of laughter and music. There was a new feeling of ease and freedom in the Lawrence household, but above all, a sense of permanence, as if his family had been wandering in the desert for a long time and had finally found its way to a safe oasis.

Although Reeve hadn't seen much of Belinda except at the dinner table, he had been keeping close tabs on her through Quincy and the children. He received daily glowing reports from both his housekeeper and his children about Belinda's magical powers as a nanny.

Not that he'd been avoiding her, he told himself as

he drifted toward the sound of the music. He'd been busy catching up with his work now that he didn't have the constant worry of finding and keeping a good nanny for his children.

Light and music poured through the open doorway, and it seemed that his den had been transformed into a place of enchantment. When he reached the door, he saw Belinda, draped in scarlet chiffon and rhinestones, her arms lifted gracefully over her head, waltzing and twirling. He watched in silent secret admiration.

Whirling slowly, she came face-to-face with him. "Hello." Her smile was radiant. "Fancy meeting you like this."

Before he could say anything, she drifted off in a whirl of chiffon skirts. Graceful as wind in the willows, she danced with the music until she had made another circuit of the room. When she was even with him once more, she paused, arms still lifted over her head.

"Well, hello again." Her voice was breathless from so much dancing.

Reeve's gaze lingered on her face, then moved to the soft blue-veined skin of her upper arms. He could see her pulse beating there, like tiny wings of a trapped butterfly. He couldn't seem to take his eyes off that vulnerable spot.

"Here it is, this lovely summer evening—" her voice wove itself around his mind, drawing his attention back to her face and her wonderful vampish lips "—and the children are all tucked into bed. Quincy's sound asleep, too. Don't you think this is a grand time to dance?''

She waited for his response. It was a long time coming. He was trapped in the contemplation of her lips.

''I suppose...'' he finally said, leaving the sentence adrift among the haunting strains of music.

Belinda took his hand and pulled him into the den. A warmth spread through him, and he reached back and quietly shut the door.

''What is that music you're playing?''

''An old Hank Williams tune, 'Your Cheatin' Heart.' It was the first record I ever owned, and I was always a fool about it. Couldn't bear to leave it behind, so when I left Augusta, I tucked it into my suitcase.''

He had a sudden vision of Belinda walking sideways under the weight of her possessions. She had tucked a Hank Williams record into her suitcase. He wondered if she'd put in her grocery-store china with the blue chickens around the border.

''Hmm,'' he murmured. Whether he was agreeing with her decision to bring her music to Tupelo or just making a noise to let her know he was listening, he didn't know. He glanced down at their entwined hands, hers as soft as a downy baby duck nestled closely in his. Holding her hand felt good and right somehow, so he held on.

''Do you dance?'' she asked.

''Not much.''

She laughed. ''That's what I figured. Shoot, I'll bet you haven't danced in a month of Sundays.''

"Something like that."

They had been moving slowly toward the center of the room as they talked. Her chiffon skirts whispered against his trousers and her fragrance drifted around him. Roses. He inhaled deeply. Nothing was so soothing as the scent of summer roses.

The music drew to a close, and Belinda released his hand. He felt deprived.

"You wait right here," she said. "Now don't you move."

He wouldn't have moved if an elephant had suddenly come in and prodded him with its tusks.

Belinda started the record again, and Hank Williams's sad song of lost love filled the room. Belinda came toward him, singing along. She had a sweet clear voice that set his skin a-tingle.

She drifted into his arms and it seemed only natural to hold her there. He didn't know who made the first move, but suddenly they were dancing, hips pressed close, hands tightly clasped. It seemed he had never danced before and, at the same time, that he had *always* danced. Belinda was tall and willowy, and she moved in his arms with more grace than any woman he'd ever known. His own movements were surprisingly sure, as if the memories of dance had been buried deep inside and had sprung to life in that moment of music and roses.

He felt something soft against his cheek and, looking down, saw that it was her hair. Belinda had laid her head on his shoulder, and her silky hair caressed his cheek. He closed his eyes to the lovely sensations that rippled along his skin.

"You dance a lot better than Charlie Crocket," she said.

"I'm glad." His hold on her tightened. He wanted her close enough so their heartbeats blended, though why he should wish such a thing was a mystery.

"Better even than Matt Hankins."

"Who's Matt Hankins?"

"Just somebody who drifted out of my life the same way he drifted in. Men seem to come and go in my life with the regularity of tides."

Reeve was jealous of them all—Matt Hankins and Charlie Crocket and every other man who had ever drifted close enough to be a part of Belinda's life. The force of his feeling startled him, and he was suddenly very conscious of the way he was holding Belinda. Like a lover.

He eased his hold and stepped back so he could no longer feel her heart's soothing rhythm against his chest. She tipped her face up and smiled at him.

"I'm harmless, Reeve."

Her quick assessment of his motives startled him. "Perhaps I'm not."

"Oh."

Her mouth tempted him, but he resisted. Gazing down at her, he lost track of the music. His steps slowed, then stopped altogether.

The music wound to a close, and still they stood in the center of the room, holding each other, locked together by mysterious urgings. Reeve was the first to let go.

He backed slowly away from her, his heart beating as if he had just escaped a band of cutthroats, bent on taking his money and his life. He moved to the sofa and sat down. Belinda stood silently in the center of the room, beautiful and lovely to look at.

There was an unconscious elegance about her that struck Reeve as both natural and surprisingly strange. How could a woman of her background project such a stately well-bred image? What would she be like if she were groomed and tutored and polished? It boggled the mind.

"Do you like ballet?" he asked suddenly.

She smiled, then came toward him, her skirts whispering softly. "Well, I've never seen the real stuff, up on a big stage and all that, but I've seen some on the TV."

With an ease born of self-confidence, Belinda sat on the sofa beside him, spreading her skirts carefully, then taking time to bend down and smooth her stockings.

Reeve rammed his hands into his pockets and cursed the impulse that had made him stay. Still, he was not a man who backed away from a challenge, and the whim that had overtaken him began to solidify into a real plan.

"Did you like what you saw, Belinda?"

"I thought all that jumping around was right graceful, and the women's costumes were just peachy, but

I did think the men ought to wear a different kind of pants. I mean, just look what all they were showing."

"Indeed." Reeve smoothed his hand over his chin to keep from chuckling. Belinda's point of view never failed to delight him.

"What would you think about going with me to the ballet Saturday night?"

"Why...I would think that was just about the grandest thing I've done since I came to Tupelo."

She leaned down to give her stockings another smoothing. Reeve's gaze followed her hands. A muscle worked in his jaw, and sweat beaded his upper lip. Someday he might have to tell her what her unconscious gesture did to him. On the other hand, he didn't really want her to stop.

Belinda finished arranging her stockings and smiled at Reeve. "Now that I'm drawing such a fancy salary, I might start going to all sorts of highbrow stuff like the ballet. I've always thought I'd like it better than mud wrestling, anyhow."

"Mud wrestling?"

"Charlie Crocket used to be right fond of the Saturday night mud wrestling. Of course, I always did like to be in a crowd that's having fun, but seeing folks grabbing at each other all covered in mud didn't have much appeal to me."

"I think you'll find the ballet much more to your liking."

The scent of roses drifted Reeve's way again, and he fought the urge to slide his arm along the back of

the sofa and rest it lightly on Belinda's shoulders. It
was time for him to go. After all, he had made a small
start on his project, and the things he wished to accomplish couldn't be done in a single evening. The
education and sophistication of Belinda Diamond
would take a long time.

Reeve smiled. He couldn't remember when he had
been as excited over a project. Belinda had great potential, and when he finished with her, she'd be the
envy of every woman in Tupelo—and the target of
every man. That last thought shook him a little. Not
for any personal reasons, he assured himself. Not at
all. His reasons for remaking Belinda Diamond were
strictly business. She was the best nanny he had ever
hired, and with a little polish, she would be perfect.
And if his finished product attracted the attention of
men, he'd just have to protect her. It was that simple.

He was enormously pleased with himself, so
pleased that he reached over and lightly squeezed her
hand.

"Will you please excuse me, Belinda?" He wanted
to get started right away lining up the necessary people
for his project.

"Certainly."

He stood up. "Thank you for the dance."

"Next time we'll do the jitterbug. It's one of the
best dances ever invented."

"Indeed." He was spellbound for a moment, lost in
thoughts of doing the jitterbug with Belinda. Then he
bade her a formal good-night and strode from the den,

trying all the while to stay in his dual role of employer and tutor.

In the doorway, he stopped and glanced back at Belinda. She lifted her hand and flickered her fingers at him.

"Toodle-oo," she said.

Reeve left the den whistling. He guessed an employer might whistle on occasion. What was the harm?

Belinda sat on the sofa, humming, watching him go. Boy, had he surprised her. That man was some dancer. Why, she had felt like she was floating, the way he had held her in his arms and guided her around the room—just floating off on a fine big old cloud.

"Hmm..." She hugged herself and closed her eyes. "My, my," she murmured, remembering how his eyes had gotten all bright and hot-looking when they had stopped in the middle of the dance and stood gazing at each other. And just to think he had invited her to the ballet....

She imagined herself walking into the auditorium, holding his arm like a queen. Why, she'd bet every woman in town would envy her. Never in all her life had a man like Reeve Lawrence drifted her way.

She leaned her head back on the sofa and imagined holding hands with him there—and even kissing him good-night. Her dream was so real she could almost feel his lips on hers.

"Hmm," she said again, then suddenly sat up, eyes wide. "Now wait here just a minute, Belinda Stubaker. This is the best job you've ever had. Don't you dare go messing it up with silly notions of falling in love with the boss.''

She got up and hurried across the room to put on some more music. Music was just what she needed to set herself straight on the present situation.

Another sad country song began, and Belinda slowly started to sway. She had done well this evening, getting Reeve to loosen up a little and dance. But that was all she planned to do—loosen him up a little and teach him how to enjoy life. Shoot, she wasn't about to overstep her bounds and find another man drifting out of her life. She was ready for a little permanence.

"I surely do love this grand house," she whispered as she twirled to the music of Waylon Jennings.

Reeve had never intended to go shopping for a dress, but that was exactly what he found himself doing the day after he invited Belinda to the ballet. He had been walking down Main Street after lunch, enjoying the sunshine and taking a rare leisurely stroll before going back to his office at Lawrence Enterprises, when he had spotted the perfect dress for Belinda. He went inside the store.

Maureen, who remembered him from the days Sunny had been alive, hurried to meet him. "Can I help you, Mr. Lawrence?"

"Yes. The dress in the window, Maureen...do you have it in size..." Suddenly Reeve paused. He had no idea what size Belinda wore. Sunny had been a perfect size six, and while Belinda was just as slim, she was also taller.

Maureen was quick to see his dilemma. "Perhaps if you will describe the lady in question, I can help you with the size."

"She's tall. At least five nine, perhaps five ten. And very slender, almost as slim as Sunny."

"I see." There was no disapproval in Maureen's tone, only a polite interest and perhaps a mild curiosity. "This dress is fitted. Is she full figured?"

"No, I wouldn't say so."

Reeve was surprised at how easy it was to shop for Belinda. He had no haunting visions of Sunny, no feelings of guilt. He didn't even suffer the dull aching sense of loss that had been a part of his life for the past two years. Instead, he felt a sense of peace as pleasant memories of times spent in this store with Sunny played through his mind. He felt almost as if he was finally bidding goodbye to Sunny, allowing her to move on to a different realm. Not that he had stopped loving her. He would never stop loving her. But now, he could let her go.

The changes had taken place so gradually he hadn't even noticed them. Time had healed his wounds. Time and perhaps a woman named Belinda Diamond.

He felt curiously buoyant, as if he might take wing and fly out of the store, holding the party dress in front of him like an offering.

Maureen got the dress for him, assuring him that the lady could return it if it didn't fit.

"Do you want it gift wrapped?"

He hadn't planned to, but gift wrapping suddenly seemed like a wonderful idea. Belinda was the kind of woman who would love a surprise that came in a fancy package.

"Yes, please. And, Maureen...use the fanciest paper you have and tie it with the biggest bow."

Maureen quirked one eyebrow upward, perhaps remembering that Sunny had been discreet and understated in all things—including gift-wrapped packages.

"Certainly, Mr. Lawrence."

Reeve considered leaving the package on Belinda's bed and letting her find it on her own. Then he thought about presenting it to her at the dinner table in the presence of his children. For a while he was taken with the idea of having it delivered to the house by a messenger boy. "Package for Miss Belinda Diamond," the delivery boy would say. How Belinda would love that!

In the end, though, he decided to be selfish and present the gift to her in a private ceremony.

That evening, he sat quietly through dinner, watching and marveling at the rapport between Belinda and the children.

"Can we show Daddy our secret now?" Betsy said in a loud whisper as she leaned toward Belinda.

"After dinner," Belinda told her. Her glance slid toward Reeve. He smiled. His life had taken on an order and a routine that was exceedingly pleasing to him.

"And what is this big secret, sweetheart?"

"If she tells, it won't be a secret," Mark chimed in.

"Can we skip dessert, Daddy?" Betsy bounced up and down in her chair, clapping her hands. "Can we?"

"If this big secret is waiting until after dinner, I suggest we adjourn to the den. We can have dessert later."

Betsy and Mark jumped out of their chairs and scampered out of the room, laughing and chattering. "We'll meet you in the den, Daddy," Mark called over his shoulder.

"Shall we?" Reeve offered his arm to Belinda—a habit he had developed in the past few days—and escorted her to the den. She glided along beside him, tall and lovely, like a long-stemmed summer flower. He had a vision of her in her new dress. It seemed that tonight was a night for surprises.

Reeve took his customary chair in the den, and Belinda sat on the sofa and spread her skirts. He watched her, waiting for another ritual—the smoothing of her stockings. Her hair swung forward in a bright fan of gold as she leaned down and ran her hands down her legs. This time her stockings had tiny sequined diamond shapes.

A satisfied sigh escaped Reeve's lips. It was funny how these small nightly rituals soothed him. Even more mystifying was the way he looked forward to finding out what sort of decorations would adorn Belinda's stockings. Sometimes, late in the afternoons, he found himself gazing out the window of his office, wondering whether she would have hearts or diamonds or bows marching in a glittering row down her slim legs.

Thank God nobody around here could read minds. He leaned back in his chair, content.

Betsy and Mark bounded into the room, trailed by Quincy.

"Lord have mercy, Mr. Reeve," she said, puffing as she lumbered toward her chair. "Them children is enough to wear Miss Belinda to a frazzle. But she don't pay it no more mind than a billy goat. Always just as lively as if she'd come up from eight hours' sleep on a feather comforter." She fanned herself with her apron. "I never seen a woman take to a job the way she's done." She smiled over at Belinda.

Reeve laughed. "Didn't I tell you, Quincy? Belinda's job is permanent."

"Ain't nothin' never been permanent with you before, Mr. Reeve. Specially where them children's concerned. I just thought I'd get my two cents' worth in. That's all."

"Point taken, Quincy." He hugged Betsy close as she sidled up to him. "Now, sweetheart, what's this big surprise you and Mark have been keeping for Daddy?"

"This." Betsy pulled a willow whistle from behind her back.

Mark came forward with his whistle. "And guess what? Belinda helped us make them!"

Reeve inspected the whistle. It was a small willow flute, ingeniously made.

"You keep surprising me, Belinda. You're a woman of many talents."

"Shoot. It's just a little old whistle. Daddy taught us how to make them down in Georgia. See, we didn't have money to spend on fancy toys and stuff, so we had to make do with what we had. Anyhow, that's not important. The important thing is I always remembered my daddy showing me how to make that whistle and the good times we had picking out tunes. I just think it's good to really be a part of children's lives."

She paused, her cheeks flushed, then turned to Betsy and Mark. "Are you ready for the show, children?"

Betsy and Mark stood side by side in front of Reeve's chair, their faces important-looking, and lifted their flutes to their lips. At first he couldn't tell that the sounds they were making were music; but gradually he began to distinguish the tune. They were playing a shaky but enthusiastic rendition of "Yankee Doodle."

As he listened to the music, a part of his mind was occupied with the things Belinda had said. She was a very wise woman. And he had set himself up as her teacher. The wonderful irony was that it appeared *he* was the one learning most of the lessons.

He was both amused and proud. With raw material

like that, there was no telling what he could accomplish.

The children finished their song; then everybody had dessert. When it was time for the children's baths and bed, they kissed their father good-night, then Belinda took their hands and excused herself.

She was halfway across the room before Reeve spoke. "Belinda." She paused, glancing over her shoulder. "I'd like to see you after you've tucked the children in."

"In your office?"

"No. Here."

"Certainly." She nodded and left the room, the children in tow.

After they had gone, closing the door behind them, Quincy settled back into her chair and gave Reeve a sassy grin.

"What was that for, Quincy?"

"You like her, don't you?"

"She's the best nanny I've ever had."

"I wadn't talkin' about no nanny. I'm talkin' personal."

"Sometimes you talk too much, Quincy."

"I'm seein' developments, and I'm likin' what I see."

"If you're putting two and two together and getting *family,* you can get that thought out of your mind."

"I ain't sayin' what I'm puttin' together." Quincy grinned.

"Good." Reeve gave his faithful old housekeeper

what he considered his best I'm-the-boss look. Because she was not the least bit impressed, he added, "My relationship with Belinda Diamond is strictly business—and that's all it's ever going to be. I don't intend to lose a good nanny."

"No, indeedy." Chuckling, Quincy rose laboriously from her chair. "I'm goin' to bed." She lumbered across the room, then turned for one last comment. "Sure does get lonesome, just one in a bed."

Reeve declined to comment. He knew Quincy would have the last word, anyway.

He sat in his chair for a moment after Quincy had gone, smiling to himself. His gift was tucked in the entertainment center, out of sight. He glanced around the den and suddenly decided, *Why not?*

He put a good blues tape on the stereo, took out a bottle of wine and turned the lights down low. Then he sat down in his chair to wait for Belinda Diamond.

Chapter Six

After the children were settled into their beds, Belinda made her way back down the vast hallway toward the den where Reeve waited. What in the world did he want to see her about? Had she done something wrong? He hadn't acted like it, and she couldn't think what it might be.

No use expecting the worst, she told herself. Then she lifted her chin and tried to think positively. Maybe he wanted another dance lesson.

She eased open the den door, expecting to see the lights blazing just the way she'd left them. Instead, she had to stand in the doorway and adjust her eyes to the gloom.

"Reeve?"

"Over here."

He was still in the chair where she had left him, but

he had been a busy man since she'd been gone. Soft blues music filled the room, and in the semidarkness she spotted two crystal wine goblets on the coffee table, catching the lamplight.

"Well, I'll be..." she said as she walked into the room.

"Please close the door behind you."

She eased the door shut, as if any loud noise might disturb the setting he had created. Then she stood uncertainly just inside the doorway.

Reeve stood up, tall and handsome and formal. "Won't you please sit down, Belinda?"

She wasn't about to be intimidated by circumstances. Walking so her skirts would swish, she made her way to the sofa.

"Don't mind if I do." Once she was seated, she leaned back, kicked off one shoe and tucked her leg under her. "My, my. How good it is to relax after a long hot summer day."

Reeve chuckled as he sat back down. She guessed that was a good sign. It did seem to her that he laughed more than he used to. She liked to think it was her influence. Maybe it was time for that jitterbug lesson she'd promised him. And after that, she thought she'd start planning family picnics. Of course, she wasn't really a part of the family, but as the nanny, she would certainly go along. And she could pretend.

She'd done a lot of pretending lately. Just the night before she had pretended Betsy and Mark were actually her children and that she would be in a front-row seat when they graduated from high school. Shoot, she could picture herself sitting in the front pew of the church when Betsy got married, wearing a nice crepe-de-chine dress with just a touch of sparkle on the shoulder. She did love fancy clothes. She gave a long contented sigh.

"Happy?" Reeve's voice startled her. He had been quiet so long she had almost forgotten he was there.

"Yes." She started to add she was happier than a pig in the sunshine, but she had noticed that Reeve didn't talk like that. She guessed if she lived around him long enough she might get to talking classy like him.

"I'm glad." He didn't say anything else, but kept watching her like she was some sort of prize at the county fair, and he was figuring out whether she was worth trying to win.

She didn't mind. In fact, she sort of liked having his eyes on her. It made her feel soft and liquid and kind of hummy inside, like she might break out in song in a minute or two.

"You've been with us two weeks, Belinda."

"So I have."

"You've done an excellent job."

"Thank you."

His eyes settled on her once more, and she let out a big sigh. "I have always believed in rewarding excellence," he said after a moment.

"That's not necessary. My salary is more than generous."

"Indulge me." Smiling, he rose from his chair. The lamplight slanted across his cheekbones, softening his whole face. Belinda wanted to leave her comfortable place at the sofa and run her hands down the sides of his face. What had come over her lately?

His back was turned to her as he fiddled about the entertainment center. It was a lovely back, proud and straight with a broad set of shoulders that made her glad he belonged to her. Of course, he didn't really *belong* to her, but he *was* her boss and she reckoned that gave her some privileges.

When he turned around he was holding the prettiest box Belinda had ever seen. "Oh," she sighed. It was a large box wrapped in gold paper and tied with a sparkly pink bow. The bow glittered so much in the lamplight that she figured it must be sprinkled with stardust.

Reeve slowly walked toward her, holding the box out in front of him. "For you," he said, setting the box on the coffee table.

"For me?"

She didn't dare touch it yet, for she couldn't believe that such a beautiful thing was hers just because she'd been in the household for two weeks. It didn't make sense to her. Nobody had ever given her such a gift.

"This is my way of saying thank you for a job well done."

She reached for the box, then ran her hands lovingly over the ribbon.

"It's so pretty I hate to unwrap it."

"I'm glad you like the wrapping." He chuckled. "But I also want to know if you like what's inside the box."

Belinda carefully removed the bow and set it aside. Then she undid the paper with equal care, folding it neatly and putting it beside the bow. She thought she'd save the wrapping forever, preserve it in a spot of honor next to her Hank Williams record.

When she saw the dress, she tried to contain her disappointment. It didn't look like much in the box, plain as could be, though it was a good color—black. Belinda had always been partial to black. She held it up and tried to sound excited.

"My, my. How elegant."

She figured Reeve was fooled, for he beamed at her as if he had invented Christmas. "Simplicity is always elegant. Why don't you try it on?"

She nodded and left the room, carrying the dress, the box and all the wrappings. Of the three, she valued the wrappings most. When she reached her bedroom she spent considerable time trying to figure out how the dress went. It was slashed in places she'd never seen slashed, and she made two or three false starts in trying to get into it.

Finally she figured it out. It came off one shoulder in the front, and most of the back was cut away. The fitted skirt buttoned straight down the back side of her left hip. First she looked down at herself, then she twirled in front of the mirror.

"Oh my!" For all its plainness, the dress was grand.

It made her look like one of those TV heroines who walk down the staircase with everybody looking. Her stockings with the rhinestones set it off perfectly, even if she did say so herself.

For a minute she thought it needed a necklace and two or three bangle bracelets and maybe her big rhinestone earrings; then she changed her mind. She walked to the dresser and took out a box she always carried with her. Inside was a pair of pearl-and-rhinestone earrings that had belonged to her grandmother. She had never worn them, for they had always seemed wrong with all her outfits; but with this dress, they looked just right.

She gave one last glance in the mirror before she left the room. She would say one thing for that Reeve Lawrence—he certainly did know how to dress a woman.

Reeve stood up when she walked into the room. An entrance like Belinda Diamond's demanded standing. She was sensational. Her creamy skin glowed against the simple black silk, and the pearl earrings she was wearing added just the right touch of elegance. Even the rhinestone-studded stockings seemed right.

"Well?" she said, twirling slowly.

"I'm speechless."

"Good. I never did like a talkety man."

Belinda paraded up and down the room as if she were a model on a runway, turning this way and that, giving him a view of herself from all angles. And every angle he saw was delicious.

He poured himself a fortifying drink of wine. When she glided his way, he offered her a glass.

"Won't you join me?"

"Well..." She caught her lower lip between her teeth. "Since this is a celebration—my two-week anniversary and all—I guess one little glass won't hurt."

She took the glass bravely and began to sip. Reeve watched in fascination as her face flushed and she sank languidly onto the couch. As the blues music drifted around them, the one shoulder on her silk dress slid downward. She hiccuped softly.

"My goodness." She giggled. "I feel all swimmy-headed."

"Perhaps you shouldn't finish that wine." He reached for the glass.

"Nonsense. I always start what I finish." She took a big gulp, and her strap slid inexorably farther.

Reeve cursed himself for being a fool. She had told him the effect wine had on her. Why had he offered her a glass? Indeed, why had he set the room up like a seduction trap, then waited inside like some love-starved teenager for his first victim?

"Hell." He sat on the sofa beside her and leaned over to pull her dress back onto her shoulder.

She leaned close to his face. "Hello, there. Fancy meeting you here." She hiccuped once more, then gulped down the rest of her wine.

Her lips were so close, so temptingly close. With one finger he reached out and traced their bow-shaped lines. They were still damp from the wine. He knew exactly how they would taste. His finger played over her lips once more. She closed her eyes and moaned.

What had he done? He jerked his hand away and began to straighten her dress. His fingers encountered her naked shoulders and he was lost once more. He couldn't seem to move. Ever so slowly, his thumbs caressed her silky skin.

"Hmm," she murmured. "Tha's nish."

She was drunk. On one glass of wine. He held her by the shoulders and gazed down into her face. Belinda Diamond was at his mercy. He could kiss her. He could pull her onto his lap and run his hands down the length of her slim legs, tracing the same path he's seen her trace so often. He could bury his face in her hair and feel its silky strands caress his cheek.

The heat of passion rose in him and he was sorely tempted. He battled temptation for several minutes, with Belinda Diamond soft and pliant under his hands. *Don't be a fool,* he told himself. A muscle ticked in his tight jaw as he carefully rearranged her dress and propped her on the sofa.

"Wait here, Belinda," he said, although the instructions were totally unnecessary. In her condition she couldn't have moved if she had wanted to. Apparently she was extraordinarily sensitive to wine, perhaps even allergic. All the way to the kitchen he berated himself. What had he been thinking of, setting out a glass of wine for her?

As he prepared a cup of strong coffee, he decided that the remaking of Belinda Diamond was going to be somewhat dangerous. She was warmhearted and sweet and sexy, and he was, after all, a man—one who had been without a woman for a long time. He'd have to learn to keep the proper distance. Surely he could exercise that much control over himself.

When he returned to the den, he propped Belinda into the crook of his arm and held the coffee cup to her lips.

"Sip, Belinda... That's right...."

She made a face. "It's bitter."

"I know, sweetheart. That's how it has to be."

Neither of them noticed the endearment. He was too preoccupied and she was too tipsy.

He held her while she finished the coffee. Then he smoothed back her hair. "Can you walk, Belinda?"

She smiled at him, then reached up and patted his face. "You're a nice man."

"Upsy-daisy." He got her to her feet. She swayed toward him and he braced her with a firm arm around her waist. "Hold on. Let's see what those legs can do."

She was rubbery-legged all the way across the den and back.

"Whoops," she said, giggling, as she fell into him.

"This doesn't seem to be working." He untangled her and tried one more circuit of the room. She spent most of the time lurching into him, hanging on and giggling.

"Are we going to dance like this all night?" she asked.

"Absolutely not."

Reeve got her into his arms and strode from the den. He had gotten her into this condition and now he was going to take care of her. There was no need to torture her the rest of the evening with strong coffee and forced marching.

Belinda wrapped her arms around him and buried her face in his neck as he ascended the stairs. He tightened his jaw and kept his inexorable march toward her bedroom.

She had left a lamp glowing beside the bed. He stepped through the doorway and kicked the door shut behind him, just in case. He never knew when Quincy would decide to roam the halls, checking on things, and he certainly didn't want her to see what was going on. She would take great delight in misinterpreting the entire scene.

Belinda moaned softly as he lowered her to the bed. She lay on the silk coverlet like a fallen flower. With the lamplight gilding her hair and her skin, she was exquisite.

Reeve yielded to temptation long enough to lean down and caress her cheek.

"You are so beautiful," he whispered.

"Hmm." She settled into a comfortable position and her eyes slowly drifted shut.

Reeve briefly considered removing her dress so she would be more comfortable, then tucking her under the covers, but that was too much temptation for any man. He contented himself with sitting at her bedside a while, watching to be sure she was all right.

She sighed and stirred in her sleep, and the smell of roses drifted around him. Once more he leaned down to caress her face.

"Do you have any idea how desirable you are, Belinda Diamond?" he whispered. *Probably not.* Once more he was overcome with the temptation to remove her dress, but this time he wasn't thinking of her comfort....

He lowered his head to his hands and groaned, then stood up to leave. The fates would just have to take care of Belinda, for he was in no condition. Belinda's discomfort and a hopelessly wrinkled dress were small prices to pay for his sanity.

Tomorrow he'd send the dress to the cleaners. And tomorrow he'd feel more like himself, more in charge. He had to, otherwise this strange metamorphosis might become permanent.

Belinda found Reeve's note when she awoke the next morning. "I've arranged to send your dress out to be cleaned and pressed. Please be ready for the ballet at seven-thirty." The note wasn't even signed.

Reeve's note crackled with cold authority. Oh, Lordy, and here she was lying on her bed still dressed in her new silk outfit. No telling what she had done after drinking the wine. The last thing she remembered was how much she wanted to crawl all over Reeve and nibble his neck.

The note was plain enough. He was going to act like nothing had happened. Maybe it hadn't. She didn't know. Anyhow, two could play the same game. Tonight when she sashayed down the stairs in her fancy new dress, as elegant as Audrey Hepburn, she'd act as cool as you please.

That evening, promptly at seven-thirty, Belinda descended the staircase. Reeve was standing at the bottom, as stiff as a stuffed turkey. Well, she wasn't going to let his attitude bother her. This was her first real ballet, and she was going to have a ball.

"Ta-da!" When she reached the bottom she twirled around for him. "I'm all pressed and polished and ready to go. How do you like me?"

"You are lovely," he said, without a smile. He held his arm out as formally as if he were a doorman or something. Belinda wanted to bash him over the head with one of her high-heeled shoes. She wanted to rumple his hair and leave a lipstick mark on his cheek and say, "Hey, let's have some fun!"

Of course she did none of those things. Instead she took his arm and inclined her head toward him as if she'd been born acting high-and-mighty.

"I'm ready when you are, master."

That brought a small smile to his face. It even put a twinkle in his eye. Good. Maybe there was hope for the evening, after all.

Once they got into the Corvette, Belinda did most of the talking. He had opened up some by the time they got to the ballet, but he said nothing personal. As they took their seats, he started explaining the ballet to her, telling her about the music and the composer, and the various places this particular company had performed.

Belinda listened with half an ear, all the while studying Reeve. He looked like a prince right out of a fairy tale. She smiled, remembering the way he had held her when they danced, recalling the way the expression in his eyes sometimes got hot when the two of them were alone together.

"You seem to be enjoying this rather boring lecture of mine."

"I am. Tell me more, please." She wasn't telling a lie exactly. What she was enjoying was the sound of his voice and the feeling of sitting beside him all dressed up, just like a real date. He leaned closer, making a point about Tchaikovsky's *Sleeping Beauty* ballet, and his arm brushed against hers. She felt as if the night sky had opened up and all the stars had lined up to blink a message, especially for her: *Belinda Stubaker loves Reeve Lawrence.*

"Oh, no," she whispered.

"You disagree with me about Tchaikovsky's music?" He smiled. "I'm glad. Nothing is more boring than a 'yes' person."

If he only knew, she thought. She didn't disagree with him about anything. In fact, if he had said the sun was black, she'd have looked for dark streaks in it. She was that much in love.

The very thought of loving her boss horrified her. Not only was she as different from Reeve Lawrence as it was possible for a woman to be, but she was putting everything she had hoped for in jeopardy—her job, her security, her future. It just couldn't be possible, she thought in panic. When had it happened? It had sneaked up on her when she wasn't looking, that was what.

The sound of his rich voice rumbled on, and she pretended to be paying attention. Thank heaven, she thought, when at last the lights dimmed and the ballet started. Now she could think in the dark without having to pretend.

She stared straight ahead at the stage, afraid her face would give her away. The costumes were beautiful, the music grand, and the dancers graceful. She should be in heaven. Her very first ballet, and here she was locked up in her own mind with her tortured love.

Maybe it wasn't so. Maybe living a fairy-tale life in that fairy-tale house had warped her thinking. Perhaps she just *thought* she was in love.

She sneaked a peek at Reeve. *No.* He was real and her love was real. She could tell. She guessed that's why things had never worked out between her and Charlie Crocket—or Matt Hankins. She hadn't really loved either of them. They had drifted into her life and selected her, and she had gone along for the ride.

A kind fate had rescued her from Charlie and Matt. Who was going to rescue her now?

The lights came up and Reeve took her arm. "Shall we go downstairs?"

"Is it over?"

"Over? No. This is intermission."

They walked downstairs, and she was saved having to talk to Reeve by the crush of people who approached him. Apparently everybody in Tupelo knew him. If he thought her silence was strange, he didn't have a chance to comment. She stood at his side and let her mind drift. Lordy, she was in a fine mess. How was she ever going to keep her feelings secret? And keep them secret she must. There was not a snowball's chance in the Bad Place that Reeve would ever fall in love again, especially with somebody who was not in his social circle. Besides all that, she had her job to think about.

"Miss Diamond? *Miss Diamond!*"

The insistent female voice shook Belinda out of her study. "Yes," she said, trying to look pert and prepared, though she didn't have any idea who the woman was or what she was talking about.

"I asked where you went to school," the woman said.

"Just about everywhere," Belinda told her, wondering why in the world it mattered.

"I mean, what *specific* school, Miss Diamond? I can't seem to place your accent. And that fashion statement..." She stared pointedly at Belinda's rhinestone-studded stockings, though how she could see through her weighted-down eyelashes was a mystery to Belinda. Then the woman gave a false laugh. "I'm a W girl, myself."

"Lois, will you please excuse us?" Reeve took Belinda's elbow with the intention of rescuing her, she guessed. Well, she was in no mood to be rescued.

"Why, Lois," Belinda said in her best drawl. "Didn't old Reevey-boy tell you? I went to the school of hard knocks."

Lois's mouth dropped open, and as far as Belinda could tell it was still hanging open when Reeve drew her back through the crowd.

"Are you mad at me?" she said.

"No."

"Then why are you scowling?"

"I'm not scowling."

"Your face would frighten old ladies into heart attacks."

"So would that fake accent you used with Lois."

"She asked for it."

"*Reevey-boy?*"

Belinda's face flushed hot, but she wasn't about to back down—boss or no boss. "I do not intend to apologize," she said softly. "You can fire me."

"Fire you?" He stopped dead in his tracks and grasped her shoulders, oblivious to the crowd swirling around them. "*Fire* you?"

Her chin came up proudly. "That's what I said." She was shaking so hard inside she thought she might break into a hundred pieces in the middle of the concert hall. Sometimes life simply wasn't fair. All she had ever wanted was little house to call her own, and what did she end up with? Loving the wrong man and losing her job by insulting his friends.

"Do you think so little of me that you believe I'd fire you because of Lois Mease?" A muscle jumped in the side of his tight jaw.

Hope sprang to life in Belinda. "No, I think you are..." She paused, thinking of all the things he was—wonderful, magnificent, handsome, generous, sexy. Of course, she couldn't say those things to him. Not now. Probably not ever. She looked him straight in the eye. "You are a very fine man."

"Good. I think you are a very fine woman, and I have no intention of firing you." He released her shoulders, tucked her hand into his arm, and escorted her back to their seats. "Let's enjoy the ballet and forget about Lois."

"She's a hard woman to forget with all that funny-looking streaked-up hair cut like a man's and all that rouge that looked like it had been put on with a hoe. I could have said a thing or two about her fashion statement, but I didn't."

Reeve chuckled. "I think you gave her what she deserved with one succinct statement, Belinda. Though I'm not fond of being called Reevey."

"I thought it was cute. Makes you sound like some kind of machine used to trim the grass."

The lights dimmed and the curtain rose. Belinda and Reeve sat side by side, watching the ballet, thinking their separate thoughts.

After the final curtain call, they made their way back through the crowd, outside and into Reeve's car. Once they were inside the rick cocoon of leather and darkness, cruising down the street in silence, Reeve launched into the subject that had been very much on his mind. In his characteristic manner, he got right to the heart of the matter.

"Belinda, for the past two days I've been planning a project that is very exciting to me."

"Good. Tell me about it." She was feeling expansive now that she had survived the threat to her job. In her present mood, she also believed she could handle her ill-fated love.

"I have already lined up all the people necessary to do the job—tutors, an elocution coach, a finishing-school expert."

"Well, that sounds ambitious...all those people." She shifted in her seat so she could see his face better in the dim light. "Now, if you'll just tell me what this project is, maybe I can offer an opinion. I have one on just about everything."

Reeve laughed. "That's the reason I decided on this project, Belinda. You are such a remarkable woman— and you have so much potential."

Belinda went very still. *She had so much potential.* Her heart hammered in her chest so hard she thought she wouldn't be able to get her breath.

"I am the project?" she whispered.

Reeve was so caught up in his plans he didn't notice her turmoil.

"Just think, Belinda. With the right tutoring you can be one of the most outstanding women in the city, even in the state."

"The ballet tonight—that was all part of the project?" Her visions of romance vanished like wisps of smoke in a strong wind.

Something in her voice made Reeve glance her way. Her face was white and stricken, as if a light had been snuffed out somewhere inside her. His hands tightened on the wheel and he silently cursed himself. In his usual bulldog method, he had plowed ahead with his "project," never stopping to think how Belinda might view it.

"Of course the ballet was not a part of the project." That was a half-truth, but maybe it would help rectify his terrible mistake. "I wanted you to see the ballet, and I needed a companion."

"Why didn't you take Quincy? I'll bet she'd love it. She might even have more *potential* than I do."

"Belinda..." She shifted as far from him as possible, hugging the door as if she were trying to disappear into the leather. "I'm sorry. I've handled this badly."

"You don't have to apologize. You think I have potential, and I guess I ought to be flattered. Some of my bosses have thought I was too independent and sassy to have potential."

"This is not about my being the boss and you being the employee." He stared straight ahead, trying to keep the anger out of his voice and failing miserably.

"Then maybe you'll tell me what it is about. See,

since I need a tutor and an elocution coach and a finishing-school expert, I'm having a hard time figuring this thing out. Maybe I need a brain transplant, too. Do you know any good surgeons?''

Belinda was past caring about her job. There would always be other jobs. Her pride had been deeply wounded. Every word Reeve said confirmed what she had always known: they were from two different worlds. And it hurt like the devil to think he believed she had to be reshaped before she was even worthy to *work* in his world, let alone love.

She clenched her hands into fists, fighting to hold back the tears. She wouldn't let him see her cry. Crying should be private, especially since she would be crying over an impossible love.

''Belinda—''

''So fire me.''

''If you say that one more time—''

He clamped his jaws together tightly and drove with a single-minded vengeance. Belinda sat on her side of the car in blistering silence.

By the time they reached his neighborhood, Reeve had calmed down enough to be rational.

''Belinda, look. Please forget the whole thing. Forget the project. Forget everything I said. You're an excellent nanny, and I appreciate you just the way you are.''

''Thank you.'' She didn't dare look at him. She didn't want to see a lie on his face. It was better for her if she pretended he was telling the truth. She wanted to salvage some of her pride.

He parked the car and they walked stiffly toward the front door, side by side but not touching. Belinda wondered why she had ever believed they would exchange a good-night kiss. Maybe she needed that tutor, after all. Maybe she needed *six* tutors.

Inside the door, she turned to face him, her hands folded in front of her, the way a good obedient employee should. "Thank you for taking me to the ballet, Reeve. Good night."

Reeve thought of a dozen things he should say, but he didn't quite know how to say them. In the end he settled for a simple good-night.

He watched her walk up the staircase. Twice he almost called her back. He had hurt her terribly, wounded her pride, probably shaken her self-esteem. If only he had explained his intent. If only he hadn't called her a project. If only he had *asked* if she was interested in being made over.

Slowly he followed her up the staircase, far enough behind so she wouldn't notice, thinking all the while that two of the saddest words in the English language were *if only*.

Chapter Seven

Belinda made it to her bedroom before the tears started. She closed the door softly, resisting the urge to slam it. When she was upset, she loved to slam things and throw things. But this wasn't her house; it wasn't her door.

She stalked across the room, tears streaming down her cheeks, and kicked the love seat. That made her toe hurt just enough to give her a reason to cry. She wanted a reason to cry besides the real one. She didn't even want to think about all her real reasons for crying.

She stripped off her clothes and stalked toward the bathroom. Reeve's words echoed in her mind: *You have so much potential.* She clamped her hands over her ears to shut them out, but she still kept hearing them.

"What's the use?" She uncovered her ears and let herself replay their conversation in the car while she drew a tub of water. Of course, she'd had one bath already this evening, but she'd always believed the best therapy in the world was a good hot bath.

When the water was almost up to the rim, she stepped into the tub and sank so low the water lapped her chin. Her hair was getting wet, but she didn't care. What did a wet head matter when the man she loved thought she needed remaking?

"Damn him!" She scrubbed hard at her face, removing all trace of tears. She didn't want to cry over Reeve Lawrence. She hadn't cried over Charlie Crocket and she hadn't cried over Matt Hankins. But she hadn't been in love with them, either.

Closing her eyes, she rested her head on the cold porcelain rim of the tub. "Be sensible, Belinda," she told herself. Oh, Lordy, she had been anything except sensible tonight. She had let her feelings take charge of her brain, and then she had let her tongue run wild. That was the thing about her—she'd always had a habit of saying what she thought. She decided it was a good thing she'd spent most of her life moving around the country, for she probably wouldn't have been able to stay put, the way she let her tongue run away with her.

Now she'd gone and done it. Tomorrow she might as well start looking for another job, no matter what Reeve had said. Working for him after all the things she'd said would be impossible.

She looked around the bathroom and sighed. All this had been hers. And she'd thrown it away in a temper tantrum. Well, not exactly a temper tantrum. But she had been mad.

She closed her eyes, and gradually the hot water worked its magic. She began to see Reeve in a new light. He *was* a wonderful man, a man who wanted only the best for his family. And tonight, she had been included in his family—sort of—and he had offered her the best.

Belinda covered her face and groaned. Why hadn't she seen the truth before? Love had blinded her. Love and pride as big as Kansas.

"Belinda Stubaker, you've been an idiot." She rose from the water and toweled herself dry. Then she rummaged in the closet till she found her snazzy pink rayon nightgown, slashed low in the back and front, and her matching pink robe. They still had the tags hanging on them. She had found them at an after-Christmas sale two years ago and had bought them for her trousseau, though at the time she didn't even have a man, let alone an engagement ring. She believed in planning ahead. Now, of course, since she had given up on the idea of marrying—especially since she couldn't have the man she wanted—she thought she might as well put on her trousseau gown and enjoy it.

A broken heart was easier to deal with when you looked your best. Belinda sat down in front of the vanity and began to brush her hair. Tomorrow morning she would apologize to Reeve, then she would ask him to drive her to Main Street and let her off.

She ran the brush through her hair, thinking of all the things she would miss: Quincy and the children, this house, this bedroom, but most of all, Reeve.

There was a soft knock at her door. She thought she must be hearing things. Nobody ever came to her bedroom door this time of night. The knock sounded again.

"Belinda?"

Oh, Lordy. It was Reeve. She laid the brush carefully aside and hurried to the door.

"Reeve?" she asked, her hand on the doorknob.

"I'm sorry to bother you so late. May I come in?"

"Into my bedroom?"

"If you aren't dressed..."

She jerked open the door. "I'm dressed."

His gaze raked over her. "So I see."

If she wasn't mistaken, his eyes lit up with that hot expression he sometimes got when he looked at her. Her legs became buttery, and she thought she might collapse. She hung on to the doorknob, gazing up at him.

"I couldn't let us part with that terrible misunderstanding between us, Belinda," he said as he came into the room.

She closed the door and stood leaning against it. "I know. I feel rotten myself."

Reeve was acutely conscious of being in Belinda's bedroom. He moved as far away from her as possible and stood with his back to the window while she hugged the door. Coming to her bedroom had been a mistake. But he wasn't about to back out now.

"Belinda, the fault was entirely mine."

"Oh, no," she said, still hanging on to the door. She had to hang on to the door, or else she might faint. Why couldn't she have discovered she loved Reeve two weeks ago? Why did it have to be tonight? If she'd had a little time to live with her love, she might have been able to handle seeing him in her bedroom. As it was, she was about to go all to pieces right in front of his eyes. She could just see herself, Belinda Stubaker, breaking into twenty-two pieces and flying all over the bedroom. She guessed her heart would land at his feet.

They were both silent for a long while, looking at each other, then they spoke at the same time.

"Belinda…"

"Reeve…"

"Ladies first," he said.

"I was mad tonight. I shouldn't have said all those things I did."

"You had a right to be mad."

"You're being too kind."

"You're being too forgiving."

Both of them gave a half smile in the way of people who are feeling a bit relieved. Belinda relinquished her hold on the doorknob, and Reeve left his haven by the window. They moved instinctively toward each other, then Belinda pulled back.

Land, what was she doing, heading Reeve's way in her pink trousseau gown like some floozy? The next thing she'd be telling him was that she loved him!

Half-angry at herself now, she retreated a step back and sat down in front of the vanity, being careful to pull her robe over her legs.

He noticed her modesty. "I probably shouldn't have come tonight. This can wait until tomorrow." He started toward the door.

"No. Wait...I just didn't want you to get the wrong idea. I didn't want you to think that I was the kind of woman who entertained a man in her bedroom—in addition to being the kind of woman who needs a whole bunch of making over."

She guessed the devil made her add that last part. Reeve's face got tight and a muscle started jumping in the side of his jaw again. Well, what did it matter when you got right down to it? She was leaving anyhow. She figured it would be easier to get over a broken heart if she didn't have to see the man who broke it every day of her life.

"Belinda, I want you to understand my motives and to understand why I took the approach I did."

"All right. I'll listen." She would try to act as graceful as possible under the circumstances, and when he had finished she might as well go ahead and tell him she was leaving. No use putting it off until tomorrow. Tomorrow wouldn't change a thing. She'd still be loving Reeve, and he'd still not be loving her back.

"I'm a businessman and I'm known for making quick decisions, then following through."

She could tell he was more comfortable now that he was discussing business matters, and that made her mad all over again. She was merely a business matter to him. She wadded a piece of her robe in her fist and squeezed it so hard she guessed she was ruining the fabric.

"That's how I approached this situation, Belinda— as a business decision." He carefully avoided calling her a project. "I sincerely thought I was doing the best thing for you, as well as for Mark and Betsy."

She hoped she didn't cry, though that was a real possibility.

"You see," he continued, "if Sunny had lived she would have taught the children about the arts, about music and literature and theater and dance and great paintings. It occurred to me that you would enjoy exposure to the arts, too, and at the same time I would be helping Betsy and Mark."

Belinda thought for a long time before she answered him. What would happen if she stayed? She had said she wanted to be a new woman and had even given herself a new name, but a person was more than a name. Reeve was offering to make her a new woman in ways that other people would notice.

"Does the offer still stand?" she asked quietly.

His smile was beautiful to see. And it broke her heart. Why couldn't he smile like that about *her* instead of about his *project*?

"Does that mean you've changed your mind?" he asked.

"Yes, I've changed my mind." She stood up so she could be tall and look him in the eye. Her daddy had taught her to look a person straight in the eye when you wanted him to know you meant business.

"Great," he said. "We'll start Monday, if that's all right with you."

"Monday's fine."

"I'll notify all the tutors."

"No."

"No?"

Land, what had she done now? She was arguing with him again, and he was her boss. She reckoned the devil had grabbed hold of her brain, or maybe it was love making her act so foolish. Well, what did it matter? It was too late to take her words back now. She might as well say what had just popped into her head.

"You're the one who wants me to learn all those artsy things.... I guess you'll be the best one to teach me."

"You want *me* to be your tutor?"

"Why not? You want me to be the pupil."

She figured he'd fire her now. She folded her hands across her stomach, waiting for the ax to fall. The room was so quiet she could hear the minutes marching by.

Suddenly Reeve laughed. Belinda felt as if a big rock had been lifted off her chest.

"Why not?" he said, as much to himself as to her. "Why not, indeed?"

"Does that mean yes?"

"Yes. Be ready for your first lesson on Monday evening."

"I will."

He bade her good-night and left the room. She turned around and faced the mirror to see if she looked any different. She didn't; it was the same old Belinda staring back at her. It seemed to her that women who had completely lost their minds ought to show it in some way, develop warts on their nose or pointed eyebrows or something to let the world know so they could run like rabbits.

She walked toward her bed, got under the covers and sighed. How was she ever going to take lessons from Reeve without showing her love?

She switched off the lamp, then just lay beneath the cool sheets staring at a patch of moonlight on the ceiling. On the other hand, at least she would be able to *see* him. If she couldn't have him, seeing him would be the next best thing.

Reeve left Belinda's bedroom, secretly delighted with the turn of events. He didn't know why he hadn't thought of being her tutor in the first place. It was logical. He was here, and he knew exactly what he wanted the finished product to be like. Why trust Belinda to the hands of strangers?

Tomorrow he would outline his plan for her transformation. When he had finished with her, Belinda Diamond would be the toast of Tupelo.

On Monday evening while Belinda supervised the children's bedtime preparations, Reeve waited in the den. He could hardly wait to get started.

Belinda came through the door, smiling and sassy. If she still felt any of the anger that had propelled them through Saturday night, he couldn't tell.

"Well, Teach," she said, "the children are in bed, so let's get started."

"Did you enjoy the ballet, Belinda?"

"Is this my first test already?"

Reeve laughed. "Impertinence will not be tolerated."

"Impertinence?"

"Sass."

Belinda sat on the sofa, folded her hands in her lap, and cast her eyes downward. "Yes, sir," she whispered with false meekness. She might have fooled Reeve completely except that she peeked up at him and grinned.

And therein lay the first stumbling block to Reeve's success: the teacher liked the student too much. He cleared his throat and tried to return to business.

"I'm going to take a scattergun approach to your lessons, Belinda."

She clutched her heart. "Do anything you want, master, just don't throw me in the briar patch." Her imitation of Brer Rabbit was perfect. And it gave Reeve his first glimpse of the way to successful teaching. Apparently Belinda was a great mimic and had an ear for language. He would not lecture her; he would *involve* her.

He pulled himself out from under Brer Rabbit's spell and carried on with the lessons. "This area is rich with the arts, Belinda. Tupelo has ballet, symphony, community theater and an excellent art gallery. We will take advantage of every performance and every exhibit. Memphis is only a hundred miles away. The Orpheum often has great productions."

"That sounds like fun, not lessons."

"Learning can be fun." Reeve stood up and began to pace. "But don't be fooled. We will discuss each artist, each composer, each play, each ballet."

Belinda loved watching him. His intensity made him very passionate. She clung to the edges of the sofa, listening and trying to keep up her lighthearted pretense. She had already been Brer Rabbit. Who could she be next? Tar Baby? Little Red Riding Hood? Chicken Little? That was it. Chicken Little. *Help. The sky is falling on my head.* Except it wasn't the sky. It was her own folly. She was the one who had asked Reeve to tutor her. But could she survive being this close to him?

He had stopped pacing and was leaning against the mantle, holding a small book in his hand. "At home we will concentrate on reading. I've made up a list for you, two books a week. You'll find all the material here in my library. If you discover you need more time, let me know. We'll work it out. Also, the books that you have already read we'll cross off the list."

She was watching him intently. He was very pleased. It seemed she planned to take this project seriously, and apparently her powers of concentration were great. He went on to explain to her that they would begin their lessons with poetry.

"Poetry is meant to be read aloud. Like great music, the pleasure is in the sound. We'll start tonight with the poems of Elizabeth Barrett Browning."

He opened a slim volume of poems and began to read. Occasionally he looked up to see the impact of the poetry on his student. Her face was rapt; and from time to time he caught a glimpse of tears in her eyes.

Nothing spurs a man on like success. Reeve read long after the lesson should have ended. He grew tired of standing and sat on the sofa beside her. Lamplight gleamed in her hair. He wanted to touch it, right where the glow of light spun its strands into gold.

He kept on reading. She leaned closer to him, her eyes fixed on his face, and he felt her skirt whisper against his legs.

"'How do I love thee? Let me count the ways,'" he read. At that moment he looked into Belinda's eyes. His heart kicked hard against his ribs. Like a man in a dream, he slowly closed the book.

"It's getting late," he said. "We'll finish this poem tomorrow night."

After she had left the room, he sat for a long time gazing at the closed door. Reeve didn't often indulge in self-analysis, but it didn't take much to know what had happened in his den tonight. He had selected love poems as Belinda's first lesson—and he had read them all to her.

He got up and carefully placed the book back on the shelf. Then he put on a cassette tape—Tchaikovsky's "Pathétique." It had been one of Sunny's favorite symphonies. The magnificent music soothed Reeve and helped him put the evening into perspective.

He was a man without a woman, a lonely man. And Belinda was a beautiful, desirable young woman. It was only natural that he should imagine he had directed the love poems to her.

He hadn't done that, though. He and Sunny had often sat side by side on the sofa on warm summer evenings, taking turns reading the words of Elizabeth Barrett Browning. Reading her work aloud this evening had brought all those memories back. He hadn't really been reading them to Belinda; he had been reliving the past.

Having rationalized his behavior, Reeve felt much better. Everything in his life was exactly the way he wanted it now: Belinda was a good nanny; the children were happy; there was a stability and sense of permanence in his home. He would do nothing to upset that balance—nothing.

Just to make certain that he kept that promise to himself, he ripped apart tomorrow's lesson plans—the love sonnets of Shakespeare—and substituted T.S. Eliot's "The Wasteland." That somber piece should keep romantic notions at bay.

Chapter Eight

As the weeks slipped by and summer turned to autumn, Belinda's education expanded to include the art of selecting fine clothes, fine foods and fine wine. In early September, Reeve directed a private showing of elegant garments in his home. The showing took Belinda by surprise, and she watched for a while in awe as he made selections.

"Belinda will need three cocktail suits," he told Maureen, who had brought out the clothes. "We'll take the red, the purple and the cream suits."

"I need only one," Belinda protested.

"You need three. The concert season is just beginning." Reeve continued making his selections as casually as if he were buying boxes of popcorn instead of expensive clothes. "The blue cocktail dress and the black one, as well."

Belinda began to panic. She moved closer to Reeve and whispered, "I can't afford all these expensive clothes."

"I'm paying." He kept riffling through the clothes rack as if money grew right along with the rosebushes in his backyard.

Belinda watched as he set aside three leather skirts with matching sweaters and four wool crepe dresses that she had thought were rather plain. She marched up to him again and tugged on his sleeve.

"I won't take them," she said, loud enough for Maureen to hear.

Reeve's expression didn't change. "Will you excuse us for a moment, Maureen? I'll have Quincy bring some coffee to you in my study."

After she had left the room, he turned to Belinda. "Whether you will take them is not a question here." He held up two dresses. "Which do you like best, the black or the green?"

"Neither. They're both plain as dirt. Anyhow, what does it matter what I like? I will not take your charity."

"This is not charity, Belinda, it's business."

All the frustrations she had kept locked inside all summer suddenly overtook Belinda. She felt as if she had walked into a box and there was no way out. If she told Reeve she loved him, she would lose her job. If she didn't, she thought she might lose her sanity.

She clenched her fists and tried to control the emotional cyclone that roared through her. It was a losing battle. Her rage at loving and not being loved back spilled out as anger over the clothes.

"I am not a kept woman!"

"That's a ridiculous notion. No one thinks of you that way."

"Maureen will. After today she'll tell everyone all over town that you bought a ton of clothes for that little upstart from Augusta, Georgia."

Reeve chuckled. "Belinda, you can be very amusing when you get angry."

"Stop patronizing me."

"That's great. I'm astonished at how quickly you learn new words and new phraseology."

She wanted to beat her fists on his chest. "Why do you always think of me as your project? I'm not a project, I'm a person."

Reeve came to her and cupped her shoulders. "I know you're a person."

His voice and his touch were kind and gentle, the sort a teacher might use with a student. His actions served only to fan the flames of her indignation.

"No, you don't. You didn't even ask if I wanted a new wardrobe."

"It's a part of your education."

"Then show me some pictures. Let me look at all those designer labels in the pages of some slick magazine from Paris, but please allow me the dignity of buying my own clothes."

"What has gotten into you, Belinda?"

"Maybe I'm in—" She bit her lower lip just in time

to keep from saying *love*. She needed a break; she
needed a change; she needed a miracle. She pressed
her hands to her temples. Like Cyrano de Bergerac—
last week's lesson—she was suffering from unrequited
love. She figured it must be the worst suffering in the
world.

"Look, Reeve, I'm sorry. Forget everything I said.
Just send the clothes back with Maureen and maybe
you can drop me off at the store next Saturday and
I'll buy one of the outfits."

She saw the muscle working in the side of his jaw.
One of the things she knew about Reeve was his bull-
headed determination to do whatever he set his mind
to.

"All right, Belinda," he finally said. "You can pur-
chase the clothes." He pulled a wad of bills out of his
pocket and pressed them into her hand. "Take this.
It's a bonus for showing Mark how to catch a fly
ball."

"That's part of my job.'

"No. It's part of *my* job. I'm his father. I wasn't
there for him—you were." He left her standing there
with the money in her hand. When he reached the
door, he turned back. "I'm sending Maureen back inside. Select whatever you wish. Just remember that we
will be attending many functions, and I want you to
be the best-dressed woman there."

"I won't take this," she said, but he had already
gone out the door.

She sat on the sofa and looked at the money in her

hand. It was probably enough to buy Louisiana, with Texas thrown in for good measure. She ought to march after him and demand he take it back.

Oh, Lordy, Belinda Stubaker. What have you gotten yourself into? She could leave. Maybe it was time to face facts. She was still only a nanny to Reeve, no matter how many new words she knew and how many fancy places she went. She'd been with him for three months now, and it seemed that he was more remote than ever. There was no hope that he would ever see her as anything except an employee in his household, somebody who helped make his life run smoothly.

But did she want to leave? Did she want to start all over again, finding another job, finding another house to live in? No. She was tired of suspense.

The door opened and Maureen walked in.

"Have you made your selections yet?"

Belinda squeezed the money in her hand. She figured that since she'd been bought and paid for, she might as well make her boss proud.

"Come in, Maureen. We'll decide together."

After the incident with the clothes, Belinda and Reeve settled back into a safe relationship—employer and employee. The concert season started, and he took her everywhere—concerts, ballets, plays, art-gallery openings, fine restaurants. People began to notice; *men* began to notice.

She got the first phone call after she and Reeve returned from dinner at one of Tupelo's fancier restaurants. He had just removed her jacket and was hanging it in the hall closet.

"Yes," she said into the receiver, "I'm Belinda Diamond. Yes. No." She laughed. Reeve paused in the act of shutting the closet door. "That sounds lovely. No, it really does, but I'm sorry, I can't."

Reeve was still watching her when she hung up the phone. He came toward her, leaving the closet door wide open. Belinda took hope from that small oversight. It was strange how a woman in love will take hope from the tiniest little thing.

"Was that a friend of yours?" Reeve asked, trying to act casual.

"No. Just someone who saw me at the restaurant tonight."

"A perfect stranger called you?"

"Yes. After we left, he inquired who we were. Then he called me." Belinda was enjoying her power. It was obvious the phone call disturbed Reeve, and she thought he needed a little disturbing. He had held the reins of power for far too long. "He sounded very nice," she added.

Reeve made a visible effort at regaining his self-control before he answered. "You have to be careful of strangers, Belinda."

"Some of the best times of my life have been had with strangers."

His face got dark and dangerous-looking, but still he held on to that iron control of his. Just once she wished he'd loosen up. It wasn't good for a man to be as tightly reined as Reeve.

He needed help, and she decided to prod him a little. "Just think of all the fun I'd have missed if I had turned Charlie Crocket down because he was a stranger."

"The man who wanted to pick your plums?" Reeve enunciated each word as if he had a mouth full of bullets and was spitting them out one by one.

Belinda laughed. "That's the one."

"And what was this man offering?" Reeve knew the phone call was none of his business. He didn't own Belinda. Still, he couldn't seem to stop himself from interfering.

"You're asking me what he was offering?" Belinda's temper ignited, and there was nothing Reeve could do or say now to save the situation. "You're asking me that? *You*, the absolute master of bribery and gestapo tactics?"

They stood in the hall, breathing heavy and glaring at each other. Rage colored Belinda's cheeks and brightened her eyes. Reeve had never found her more desirable than at that moment.

Without thinking, he grabbed her shoulders and hauled her close. Holding her tightly with one hand, he tipped her face up with the other. "Would you like to explain your accusations?"

"I think they are self-evident."

"What do you consider bribery? The dinner, the wine, the clothes?"

"Take your choice. I'm bought and paid for."

"In that case I may as well get my money's worth."

His mouth came down on hers, and he kissed her with such savage fury both of them were left breathless. When he finally let her go, he stared at her as if he had never seen her before.

She didn't dare speak; she didn't dare move. She barely dared breathe. The man she loved had just kissed her and she was in heaven—and in hell. She longed for his touch, longed for his lips on hers once more, but she wanted to be kissed with love, not with anger. *How could she endure this continued rejection?*

She had to be brave and strong. She had endured a childhood of never knowing from one day to the next what city she'd be living in, let alone what house. Shoot, she never even knew if she'd *have* a house. Many nights she and her daddy and her sisters had slept in the car.

She had a house now—and she wasn't going to give it up for unrequited love. She drew herself out of his embrace and stood facing him.

"Did you get your money's worth?" she asked quietly.

He didn't reply for a long time. She could see his struggle to regain his composure. Never had she admired him more; never had she loved him more.

"I'm sorry, Belinda. I lost my temper. It won't happen again." He turned and started up the stairs. "Good night."

She didn't even reply. With the sound of her heart

cracking into six pieces and ringing in her ears, she
stood in the hallway and watched him go. Then she
crossed to the closet and shut the door.

Reeve had meant what he said. He wouldn't lose
control again, and he wouldn't kiss her again. Maybe
the next time a man called, she'd accept the invitation.
Keeping her job didn't mean she had to give up her
social life.

Belinda felt so defeated she thought she might have
to crawl up the stairs. Her legs surprised her by holding her up all the way to her bedroom.

Adversity often brings out the best in people, Reeve
had said during last Tuesday's lesson.

"Sometimes it brings out the worst, as well," she
whispered now.

Reeve lay in bed, rigid with anger. That was all he
needed. Some man interested in a casual fling coming
along to take Belinda away from him. Just when everything was going so well.

He had shaped her and polished her, and now, when
she was sparkling like a fine diamond, some fool was
going to turn her head and talk to her about a trip
down to the Bahamas or a fun weekend in Las Vegas.
Then Reeve would be looking for another nanny for
his children. They would be heartbroken.

Besides that, Quincy would never stop berating him
for losing Belinda. In addition, he would once more
be left alone, trying to juggle work and children and

all the myriad details of his life that Belinda took care of.

He sat up and gave his pillow a vicious punch. Maybe things would look better tomorrow. Perhaps he was overreacting.

The next few days things got worse. Much to Reeve's horror, Belinda was suddenly a hot item in town. It seemed that the failed suitor had talked, and every one of his friends—and he must have had dozens—kept the telephone lines busy trying to get a date.

Reeve stood by with tightly clenched jaws, observing the emergence of his creation into the social whirl. Fortunately Belinda had the good sense to turn all the suitors down. But how long would that last? Reeve couldn't keep her in a cocoon forever. He had created a butterfly, and now it was time for her to soar.

Eventually the day came, as he knew it would, when Belinda said yes. Two weeks after their fight in the hallway, Reeve stood at his window and watched as Belinda got into the car with her date for the evening, a handsome brawny young man who must surely be all muscle and no brain.

"It's none of my business," Reeve said, turning away from the window.

He sat at his desk and took out a project he was working on. Within the week, he would be leaving for Germany, and he had a lot to do beforehand.

Pushing Belinda from his mind, he concentrated on

his work. Finally he stood up and stretched. The clock in his office chimed the hour. Belinda had been gone three hours. Good Lord, how long did it take to see a movie? That was where she'd said they were going, to a horror movie, of all things. He had been glad to know, although he had been careful not to ask.

Granted, they would probably stop for hamburgers on the way home. The young man had looked like the hamburger type to him. On the other hand, perhaps he had driven Belinda to some dark country road and parked. Did people still do that these days?

Reeve began to pace. There was nothing he could do except worry—and wait. Under the circumstances he thought it best to wait up for Belinda and warn her about men like Jerry Orion. What kind of name was that, anyway? It sounded suspicious to him, like a fictitious name. What if he had let Belinda go out with a criminal?

He looked at the clock again. Three and a half hours. He started to call the police, then realized the folly of that move.

Would she never get home? And what if she didn't? His carefully ordered life would turn into a runaway snowball once more.

Reeve made himself stop pacing and sit down at his desk. The German project seemed to glare up at him.

Suddenly he lifted the file and a new, horrifying thought came into his head. In less than a week, he would be leaving for Germany. There was no telling what would happen while he was gone. He might even come back to find Belinda engaged…or married. After all, she was the most beautiful, most desirable, most charming woman in town. Thanks to him.

He clenched his jaw. Belinda was *his*. She was his creation. For a moment, Reeve let his emotions take charge as he thought of all the awful possibilities.

Then the businessman in him took over. He had never seen a problem that couldn't be solved. He went into the kitchen and made himself a cup of coffee, then he came back to his desk and began to work out a solution to his problem.

Belinda endured her date. Not that he wasn't charming; he was. And not that he wasn't handsome; he was. He was also intelligent and thoughtful and witty. But he was not Reeve.

She figured she would go down in history as the most boring date of his life, for she spent half her time looking at her watch and the other half wondering what Reeve was doing.

Unfortunately, Jerry Orion was the kind of man who didn't need help in being entertained. She could have been a pumpkin head sitting on a mop handle, and he still would have stayed out till past midnight, having a big time.

Finally she couldn't stand the suspense any longer. She had to know what Reeve was doing. Had he gone to bed and forgotten about her? Had he waited up? If he had, what would he say? Would he be glad she was dating? Would he be mad? Would he be jealous?

"I hate to be a party pooper," she said, "but it's getting rather late."

"This night is young and so are we."

"Granted. But I have the responsibility of two children who get up early, no matter how late I've been out."

"I take it that means you want to go home?"

"Please."

"Done. They don't call me Jovial Jerry for nothing."

When they got to her front door, Jovial Jerry was satisfied with the obligatory thank-you-for-the-nice-time kiss. She was grateful.

He caught her hand. "I'd like to call you again, Belinda."

She didn't want to go out with him again, but she didn't want to hurt his feelings. She hesitated a fraction too long.

Jerry smiled and patted her hand. "Call me if you're free. I'm listed." He walked down the porch steps whistling. "Night, Belinda," he called over his shoulder.

"Good night, Jerry."

She saw light under Reeve's office door the minute she got to the hall. Her heart jumped in her chest, and she felt excited and elated and angry and hopeful all at the same time. She thought about waltzing straight over and knocking on his door, but then decided to play it cool and go upstairs.

She had her foot on the first step when Reeve

opened his door. Light poured out into the darkened hall, and she didn't have to turn to know he was there. She could *feel* him.

"Belinda."

She turned slowly, like Queen Victoria, granting an audience to a loyal subject. If she had learned anything these past few months under Reeve's tutelage, she had learned to exhibit grace under pressure.

"Yes?" she said, with just the right inflection of haughtiness.

"Would you come in here, please?"

If he hadn't added that "please" she might not have gone. But since he was being polite, she decided to oblige.

He had gone back to his desk and was sitting in his chair by the time she entered his office. That was all right with her. Keeping a distance helped. She sat in the chair facing his desk and gracefully spread her skirts around her. Then she leaned down and smoothed her stockings, making sure the rhinestone hearts were in a straight line.

For all her newfangled ways and newfangled clothes, she still clung to her stockings with the rhinestone decorations. They were as much a part of her as breathing, and Reeve didn't seem to mind. In fact, she sometimes thought he liked them, especially when he watched her the way he was doing now, with that hot gleam in his eye.

"Did you have a good time this evening?" he asked.

"Yes," she lied, studying him closely, trying to gauge his feelings. He seemed extraordinarily relaxed.

"What did you think of the movie?"

"You know me. I love all movies."

"Yes." He smiled. "I know you."

There was something strange about this interview, something unlike any of their other meetings, but Belinda couldn't put her finger on it. She became wary.

"Is there anything specific you want to talk about, Reeve?"

"Indulge me a moment—please." He actually smiled at her. She guessed that meant he was happy she'd gone out with Jerry. Maybe Reeve was even hoping Jerry would take her off his hands.

"Do you have plans to see this young man again?"

"Does my job hinge on my answer?"

"No. And please feel no compunction to answer if you don't want to."

"Since you put it that way—no, I don't plan to see him again."

Reeve smiled once more. Belinda held on to her composure, but it was hard. Keeping her love a secret from a cool and aloof Reeve was one thing; keeping it a secret from a warm and smiling Reeve was another. She folded her hands in her lap and watched him with all the quiet dignity she could muster.

Reeve fiddled with his letter opener. Such a nervous gesture was unusual for him. When he dropped it back to his desk with a clank, Belinda jumped.

"I suppose you want to get married someday," Reeve said.

Married. What was Reeve thinking? She decided to play it light. "I used to think about that a good bit, but my best prospects got away."

"Ah, yes. Charlie and Matt?" He studied her a while, then said suddenly, "Did you love them?"

"No."

"But you considered marrying them?"

"At the time I thought it was a good idea."

"I see." Reeve picked up the letter opener once more and ran his finger down the length of the blade. His eyes were dark and unfathomable as he looked at her across his desk, then very carefully he put the letter opener back down on the desk.

"Belinda, I have a business proposition for you."

"Another one?"

"Yes." He smiled again. "This time I plan to tell you my reasons before I propose the business arrangement. All I ask is that you please hear me out before you say anything."

"Agreed."

"You know that after my wife died I had a hard time keeping a nanny for the children. I lost eight of them in two years. Some of them left of their own accord. I fired the others." He paused to let that bit of information sink in.

"My household and, indeed, my very life, seemed to be out of control. I am a man who likes order and routine and a sense of permanence. I need stability and I want my children to have it, too."

He rose from his chair and stood gazing out the window at the darkness. Belinda didn't say anything. She hardly dared breathe. Prickles danced along her skin, and she developed a nervous itch on her elbow, but she didn't dare scratch it.

Reeve turned from the window and walked to her chair. Then he squatted beside her and took her hand. "Your hand is cold."

"Am I allowed to respond?"

"Yes."

"Yes, my hands are cold—and yours are warm."

"That makes us a team. I'll transfer some of my warmth to you." He took both her hands and chafed them between his. "Better?"

"Yes. Thank you."

He studied her a long time before he said anything. Having him so close made her heart flutter and her pulse race. Oh, Lordy, she loved this man. *Please don't make me do anything foolish,* she silently prayed.

"Belinda, what I am about to propose is going to sound shocking to you at first, but I want you to give it very careful consideration. You don't have to tell me your answer right away. You can give me your answer in the morning."

"The answer to what?"

He stood up and took his chair behind the desk once more. "In less than a week I'll be leaving for Germany. I've decided that the best way to ensure permanence in my household is to marry you.''

"*Marry* me!''

"This is strictly a business proposition. In return for your loyalty to me and my children, I will provide a generous income for the rest of your life and a house to be purchased for you at my death. Naturally, my children will inherit this house.'' He gave her time to digest his proposal, then he continued, "I will not expect to exert any conjugal rights. I am not buying your body, just your loyalty.''

"You have that, anyway.''

"Not as a guarantee. You are a lovely young woman, Belinda. You won't always be content to stay in my house and take care of my children. Before long some young man will turn your head, and you will leave.''

She squeezed her hands together in her lap to keep from twisting the hem of her skirt between her fingers. Her head was spinning. Here she was, sitting in Reeve's office listening to her dream come true. She should feel excited and happy. Married to the man she loved. What more could a woman ask for?

That he love her back! a small voice in her head replied. Oh, Lord, it seemed she was always wanting more than she was getting.

"If you agree to this proposition, Belinda, we will be married before the week is out. I'll arrange for all the necessary tests and legal documents tomorrow. I know this is unexpected, and you don't have to give your answer tonight, Belinda. But I would like an answer in the morning.''

"What about love?" she whispered.

"I thought I made that clear. This is a business proposition."

"I know...you want to marry me for business reasons. Did you marry Sunny for love?"

"Of course."

"Then how do I know you won't fall in love again and divorce me—*if* I decide to marry you."

"Belinda, love is well and good for the young and the innocent. I had it once, and I'm grateful for that, but I don't plan to indulge in it again. A man with a family can't build his life on emotion, but he can build it on careful planning."

"Like selecting the right stocks and investing in the right properties?"

"Precisely."

Belinda didn't like the idea of being no more than a good investment. But she liked the alternative even less—leaving and never seeing him again.

Her dream was being offered to her, and although it was only a fragment, she knew she couldn't let it pass her by. She wanted Reeve's love—that much was true. But she also wanted permanence, no matter what the price. Maybe the love would come.

"My answer is yes."

"Yes?"

"Yes, I'll marry you."

They sat gazing at each other across his desk. Somehow it didn't seem appropriate to Reeve to dismiss her, and somehow it didn't seem appropriate to Belinda to leave. Surely there ought to be more to a wedding proposal than merely the asking, she thought.

"Is that all?" she finally said.

"Yes. Of course, we could shake on it. A gentleman's agreement."

Both of them stood up, and she leaned across his desk. He squeezed her hand, then held it, studying her face.

"Is your lipstick smeared?"

"Why do you ask?"

"As your prospective husband I have a right to know. Did that man kiss you good-night? Did he touch you?"

She withdrew her hand and stepped back. "I'm sorry. I have sold my services as a nanny and a companion. You have no rights concerning my body."

With her head held high, she walked out.

Chapter Nine

Standing in the courthouse the next day beside Reeve applying for the marriage license, Belinda felt as giddy as if she were going to walk down the aisle of some small country church and pledge her vows to a man who adored her above all else. She'd always had a great gift for pretense, and somehow pretending made all this feel better.

She even slid her hand into Reeve's, just like a real bride-to-be might do. He squeezed her hand, then held on, and she started imagining that she might win his love in the next three days so that on their wedding night she would become Mrs. Reeve Lawrence in every sense of the word.

What she would have to do, of course, was run down to that little lingerie shop on the corner after she left the courthouse and get herself a new trousseau gown. She wondered what color Reeve liked. Maybe she'd ask him, and—

"Belinda—Miss Diamond." She looked up to see Reeve and the woman behind the desk in the chancery clerk's office both watching her.

"Sign here," the woman said.

Belinda took the pen and wrote her first name in bold letters. She had already started the "D" for Diamond when she realized she was signing a legal document. Oh, Lordy, the time for reckoning had come. She bit her lower lip and looked up at Reeve. What in the world would he do when he found out she had been lying about her name all along?

"Belinda, is anything wrong?"

"Yes." She laid the pen aside.

"You haven't changed your mind, have you?"

"No."

"Then tell me. What's the matter?"

"Reeve...can I speak to you alone, please?"

"Certainly."

He took her elbow and led her into the hallway. There was no one in sight except the janitor, and he was so busy with his mop and bucket, Belinda figured he'd never notice them, let alone hear them.

"I have something to tell you, Reeve."

He smiled. "If this is like that last confession you made—about using my soap—you need not look so distressed."

"Oh, it's worse than that. Much worse."

"You used the bath oil, too?" He was in a jovial mood. Belinda decided that boded well for her.

"Oh, dear," she said.

Reeve cupped her cheek with one hand and leaned closer to her. "Have I ever given you cause to be afraid of me, Belinda?"

"No."

"Then there's no need to be afraid now. Whatever you have to say can't possibly be so terrible as all that."

"It's worse than terrible. It's a downright sin."

"You need not make any last-minute confessions, Belinda. Your past life has no bearing on this marriage. It's a business proposition, remember?"

"Even a business proposition would be null and void if you married the wrong woman."

Reeve threw back his head and laughed. "You're not the wrong woman. I picked you, Belinda Diamond."

"I'm not Belinda Diamond," she blurted.

Reeve went very still, and for a minute she thought he was going to walk out and leave her stranded in the courthouse. His face changed to that impersonal mask he generally wore for her, and he stepped back.

"If you're not Belinda Diamond, who are you?"

"Belinda Stubaker."

"Do you have any other aliases?"

"No."

"Did someone send you to Tupelo? Did someone

pay you to come to my house and ingratiate yourself with my family?''

''No.'' Her eyes were bright with unshed tears, and Reeve could see that she was telling the truth. The panic he'd felt when she first told him her news began to subside. Everything was going to work out. This was merely a minor hitch.

He put his arm around her shoulder and led her to a bench along the wall of the echoing hallway. When they were seated he took her small hands in both of his.

''Why don't you tell me why you used a false name?'' He thought he knew, but he wanted to hear her tell him.

''Well...it's like this. When I left Augusta, I was determined to be a new woman. You and Betsy and Mark were the first people I met in Tupelo, and you looked so grand standing there in that big front yard that I just couldn't bear to introduce myself as the same old person, Belinda Stubaker, who had never known anything except moving from one town to the next and watching people come and go in my life.''

''So you called yourself Diamond.''

''I made the name up on the spot. I picked it because it sounded glamorous and sort of sparkly and shiny, just like I wanted my new life to be.''

Reeve pulled her close and hugged her. With one hand he smoothed back her silky hair. ''Belinda, I'm going to give you a new name—Lawrence. And I hope to make your life sparkly and shiny. We'll go places

together—you and the children and I. I'll take you to
see Paris and London and Rome. I'll buy you cars and
furs and jewels. I'll give you anything you want.''

Except love, Belinda thought, but she didn't say it
aloud. Instead she smiled up at Reeve.

"Thank you."

"You're welcome." He patted her cheek. "Are you
all right now?"

"Yes."

"Good. Then let's go back inside and sign that marriage license, Belinda Stubaker."

Three days later they were married in the rose garden behind Reeve's house with Quincy and the children as witnesses. It was a short simple ceremony, and
when the minister said to Reeve, "You may kiss the
bride," he bent down and gave Belinda a light kiss on
the cheek.

Quincy and the children didn't seem to notice, but
Belinda did. All the pretending in the world couldn't
hide the fact that Reeve Lawrence didn't love his
bride.

After the ceremony they went back inside for a family reception, just the five of them—Reeve, Belinda,
Quincy, and the children. Quincy had cooked all sorts
of goodies, and there was a festive air about the house.

"This is a happy day for this old place," Quincy
said, beaming. "Yes, sir, I'm tellin' you. We got us a
real family now."

Quincy passed around the wedding punch and cake,

then herded the children off to their playroom. "Come on here, young 'uns. Them two lovebirds needs to be alone."

"You didn't tell her?" Belinda asked when they were alone.

"I saw no need."

"What about the children? Do they know we're not a real family?"

"We *are* a real family. You bear my name now, and that's all that matters."

"There's no need to raise your voice."

"I'm sorry." Reeve drained his glass of punch, then walked to the liquor cabinet and poured himself some wine. "This is more festive," he said.

"I'll decline." Belinda sat down on the sofa. She was not in a festive mood. Besides, didn't he remember what had happened the last time she'd had a single glass of wine?

Reeve sipped his wine, watching her over the rim of his glass. He was feeling good. "You seem pensive, Belinda." He walked to the sofa and sat beside her. "Is anything bothering you?"

"No."

He was quick to see her lie. Sliding his arm along the back of the sofa so it rested lightly on her shoulder, he leaned closer.

"If you are worried about tonight, there is no need. I told you before that I will not assert my rights as a husband."

What about my rights as a wife? she thought, but

she didn't say anything. Instead she stared straight ahead, trying to ignore the pressure of his arm on her shoulder.

"You've made that perfectly clear, more than once, as a matter of fact—I heard you the first time."

"I didn't mean to upset you." Reeve was genuinely puzzled. Belinda had been perfectly calm during the three days of wedding preparations, and now that it was all over she was showing signs of falling apart. He couldn't let that happen. Tomorrow he was leaving for Germany, and he certainly didn't want to leave an unstable household behind.

"Everything's going to be all right, Belinda." He caressed her shoulder in what he hoped was a soothing manner. It only seemed to agitate her more. "I promise you that everything will be all right. Nothing has changed."

She jumped off the sofa to get away from his arm. Then, with both hands on her hips, she faced him. "What does that mean, nothing has changed? Am I your nanny or am I your wife?"

"You're my wife, of course."

"In name only," she said.

His eyes got dark, and she could see the storm clouds begin to gather in his face. *Don't let your tongue get you in trouble,* she warned herself, but it was already too late. Here she was, married only one hour, and already she was fighting with her husband.

"I thought you understood that from the beginning," he said.

"Maybe understanding it and feeling it are two different things."

Reeve stood up and caught her by the shoulders. His face softened as he studied her. "You're so young, Belinda, so very young." She bit her lip to keep the tears out of her eyes. "I suppose that like all young women you had romantic dreams of a big church wedding with all the trimmings. I'm sorry I denied you that."

That's not all you denied me, she wanted to say. But she didn't say that, either. Reeve hadn't denied her his love; he had simply never offered it. She had gone into her loveless wedding with her eyes wide open. It wasn't his fault if she wanted more than he could give.

She heaved a big sigh, then straightened her shoulders and lifted her chin. After all, she still had her pride. She *really* was a new woman now, Belinda Lawrence, with a head full of new ideas and a closet full of fancy clothes. It was high time she started acting like a real lady.

She pretended she was the star in her very own movie, and somewhere from the depths of her suffering soul, she brought up a smile. "Just look at me," she said, "acting as if I had just walked down the aisle with some cranky old fool who might tie me up in the cellar and serve me bread and water."

Reeve laughed, then released her. "I promise you all the food you want and a very soft bed."

But not your bed. She gave him another bright smile.

"You've just made all my dreams come true." She laughed with false gaiety and started toward the door. "If you don't need me for anything, I'll join the children."

"That's a good idea. Quincy probably needs some relief."

Without looking back, Belinda left her new husband standing in the den. The minute she was out of sight and earshot, she said, "So do I."

Belinda sought solace in the children, and Reeve sought solace in work. He took one last look around his den at all the party leftovers, then strode from the room, got into his car and drove to his office. He was a busy man. And now that his life was permanently in order he was going to concentrate on developing foreign markets for Lawrence Enterprises.

As he sat in his office trying to work, he got sidetracked from time to time by a vision of Belinda in the rose garden, dressed in white, saying her vows. She had been exquisite. He almost wished their vows had been pledged from the heart. He almost wished he had fallen in love again and would be going home to his wedding bed. Hell, if he really loved her, he wouldn't be at the office now. He would already have her in his bed. Touching her...kissing her...feeling her soft yielding body under his.

Sweat broke out on his brow. He left his desk and hurried to the window. The view was the same—a concrete parking lot and the small park with trees and flowers and picnic benches he had built two years ago for his employees.

Everything is the same, he told himself. Nonetheless, he stayed at his office through dinner. He stayed until it was time to tuck his children into bed.

Belinda watched at the window until Reeve came home. By the time she saw his car, she had been at the window for an hour, squeezing the side of her skirt until she was sure she had worn a hole in the fabric. Her heart set up a crazy pounding when she saw him striding up the walk. *Her husband.* She would know his walk if he were in the midst of a thousand other men.

"Oh," she said, pressing her hand over her mouth. The outside lights shone done on his hair, creating a halo effect. When he disappeared onto the porch, she left her vigil at the window and raced toward the stairs. One thought was uppermost in her mind—she had to touch him.

She reached the top of the stairs just as he came in the front door.

"Belinda?" He studied her flushed face, her clenched hands. "Is something wrong? It's not the children, is it?"

"No." She forced herself to unclench her hands and descend the staircase like a woman in full possession of her senses. "I heard your car, and I thought I'd come down and see if you needed my help…tucking the children in."

"Thank you, Belinda." She took one more step down the stairs, and he caught the glimmer of rhinestones on her stockings. That single bit of glitter almost cost him his control. Heat coursed through him and his loins tightened. She was his now, legally his. He could do with her as he pleased.

His breathing became harsh, and rising passion threatened to overwhelm him. Her foot was on the next step when he saw awareness come into her eyes. She knew. With the natural instincts of a woman, she *knew* he wanted her.

And if she came any closer, just one more step down the staircase with rhinestones hearts in a shining path on her slim legs, he was likely to throw her over his shoulder, carry her into his office and take her on his desktop. He must be going insane.

"Wait!" He didn't know he had shouted until she jumped. She almost lost her footing on the staircase.

Reeve raced to her side and hauled her up against him, a muscle jumping in his clenched jaw.

"Reeve?" She reached up to touch his face. Her hands felt as cool and soft as dewdrops. He closed his eyes and clenched his teeth over a groan. "Reeve…is anything wrong?"

His eyes snapped open. "No." He allowed himself one last hungering look at her before he let her go. "Listen, Belinda, it's late and you've had a hectic day. I know you must be tired."

"I'm never tired," she whispered, hugging her arms around herself where he had touched her.

"Nevertheless, I want you to forget about everything except relaxing. I'll handle the children."

His eyes swept over her one last time; then he turned abruptly and left her standing on the staircase gazing after him.

"Relax?" she whispered when he was out of earshot. "How in the name of all that's sacred can I relax when the sight of you tears me into a million pieces?"

She leaned over the railing as far as she dared, hoping to catch one last glimpse of Reeve, but he had already disappeared down the hallway.

They spent their wedding night staring out the window at the moon—from separate bedrooms.

The next morning Reeve had dark circles under his eyes, and Belinda was pale and wan. They didn't say much to each other over breakfast, preferring to let the children's chatter cover their silence.

Quincy paraded in and out of the breakfast room, her wise old eyes taking in everything. By the time Reeve was ready to leave for the airport, Quincy was scowling and mumbling to herself.

Reeve ignored her. He gave each of his children lengthy hugs, big kisses and instructions to be good; then he turned to Belinda and caught her hand.

"I'll be home in a week, Belinda."

"I know."

"Take care while I'm gone."

"I will."

"I've told the school principal to call you if there are any problems with the children." She nodded. "I'll be in touch, but if you need anything you have only to pick up the phone and call me—or call my office. Jim will take care of you."

He was speaking of Jim Crammer, vice president of Lawrence Enterprises. Belinda doubted that Jim could take care of her problem. There was no one in the world who could handle the problem that had robbed her of a night's sleep and was threatening to rob her of her sanity.

Reeve kissed her lightly on the cheek, then he was gone. The children hurried off to their playroom, and Belinda stood in front of the closed door, her right hand clenching and unclenching her skirt.

"You gonna wear a hole in that skirt if you don't quit worryin' it," Quincy said.

"Oh." Belinda released her skirt, then smoothed it. "I guess I'm nervous—" she smoothed her skirt once more "—with my husband leaving and all that."

"Humph. Mad is what I'd be if I was in your shoes."

"Reeve can't cancel a business trip just because he got married."

"Ain't no business trip I'm talking about. It's the weddin' bed."

"The wedding bed?"

"You know what I'm talkin' 'bout. It ain't right for

a man not to even sleep in the same room with the woman he's done pledged vows to. Ain't right a'tall.''

At that moment Belinda could have killed Reeve. Why hadn't he explained things to Quincy? Now he was off to Germany and she was left to placate the indomitable housekeeper. She decided to turn the tables.

"Have you been snooping, Quincy?"

"Humph. Didn't take no snoopin' to hear them two doors slam shut last night. It like to tore the house down. I was comin' down the hall to be sure the front door was locked, and I like to jump out of my slippers.'' Quincy shook her head. "Separate bedrooms— and on the weddin' night. It ain't right.''

Belinda felt the humiliation seep all the way down to her toes. Not getting to sleep in her husband's bed on her wedding night somehow made her seem unworthy in Quincy's eyes. It was all Reeve's fault. He should have foreseen Quincy's meddling and forestalled it with an explanation before the wedding. On the other hand...

A smile as big as Kansas lit Belinda's face. She was beginning to see wonderful possibilities in his secrecy. If only the two of them knew the marriage was in name only, what was to stop her from making it a *real* marriage? Then Quincy and the rest of the world would just think they had gotten off to a slow start.

"I was nervous, Quincy. And Reeve is a wonderful gentleman.'' She looked at the old housekeeper with new purpose sparkling in her eyes. "You know that.''

Quincy beamed. "He's the finest man alive. I ought to know, 'cause I helped raise him."

"There now. You see." She drew Quincy up the stairs. "I have a whole week to get over my shyness, and in the meantime there are some things I'd like you to help me do."

"Jest tell me what to do, and if I don't like it I'll tell you to go to the jumpin'-off place."

They laughed together.

"The first thing I want you to do is teach me to drive."

"Teach you to drive? Lord have mercy."

"Now, Quincy, get that look off your face. Tomorrow morning, after the children have left for school on the bus, you and I are going to get into your car and go out into the country for my first driving lesson. And today..." She led Quincy up the steps, outlining plans for yet another surprise for Reeve.

Belinda had her first driving lesson at ten o'clock the next morning. She and Quincy were in the housekeeper's old beat-up Ford on a wide expanse of pasture on Quincy's brother's farm in nearby Mooreville.

Belinda was at the wheel. Quincy sat beside her, calm as a summer day, and her brother, Australia, stood nearby wringing his hands and calling out instructions.

"Now watch them cows," he yelled as the Ford

careered toward one of his prize Herefords. "Stop! Stop!" He ran toward them waving his hands.

Belinda got excited and rammed the gas pedal, swerving just in time to miss the cow. The cow went bellowing off across the pasture, and the car swerved toward the lake at top speed.

"Lord, have mercy upon my soul," Australia moaned. "That fool woman is gonna get herself killed, and then it's my hide on the firin' line."

Quincy pointed out the brake pedal just in time to save them both from an unplanned baptism. "You doin' right good for a beginner," she said, her hands folded serenely across her big bosom.

"Thanks. I do believe I'm getting the hang of it." Belinda grinned. "Won't Reeve be surprised that I can drive!"

"That ain't all he's gonna be surprised about." Quincy thought about the arrangements she and Belinda had made the day before, and the more she thought the harder she laughed. Belinda joined her.

By the time Australia arrived at the car, intent on rescuing two crying women, they were nearly in hysterics from laughing so much.

"Women," he said. "I ain't never gonna understand 'em."

Reeve arrived home from Germany at midnight, one week after he had left. He let himself in the front door, then carried his bag up the stairs. He paused outside Belinda's bedroom door. She would be sleeping, her hair spread across the pillow like a bolt of silk and her long eyelashes curved over her soft cheeks.

The urge to see her was so great he put one hand on the doorknob.

Don't be a fool, he told himself. Tomorrow would be time enough to see her. And besides, what did he think he would do once he got into her bedroom? Take her into his arms and kiss her hello? Hold that perfect body next to his while his heart beat like an eagle's wings in a strong mountain wind, then turn and walk away?

Reeve set his jaw in determined lines and headed for his own bedroom. He set his bag just inside the door and stripped off his coat and tie. He was exhausted. It would be good to climb into bed.

His belt buckle rattled as he tossed his pants toward the valet and missed. He must be more exhausted then he'd thought. He'd never missed before.

He squinted his eyes, trying to find his pants and hang them up, but it was too dark. That was another thing—what in the hell were the draperies doing shut in his room? He liked moonlight streaming through the windows. It must be Quincy's doing. She was always changing little things, merely to assert her power.

Reeve thought about opening the curtains, but gave up on the idea. He was too tired even to walk across the room. Stripping off his shorts, he climbed into bed. The cool sheet settled over him.

Something stirred in his bed. Reeve stiffened.

Soft murmurings came from the other side of the bed, and the scent of roses wafted toward him.

"Reeve?" a soft voice whispered.

He sat up and snapped on his bedside light. Belinda lay stretched upon his bed, her hair enchantingly tumbled and her eyes bright with welcome.

"What are you doing in my bed?"

The light went out of her eyes. She sat up, hugging the covers to her chest.

"If you're going to shout, the least you could do is put on some clothes. I don't fancy arguing with a naked man."

Chapter Ten

"I always sleep naked—and alone," he said, not even bothering to cover himself with the sheet. He was furious, more at himself than Belinda. He had lost control. The bad part was he couldn't seem to get it back. Especially with Belinda only inches away, her gown straps slipping down her shoulders and her lips still pouty from sleep. God, how he wanted to kiss her.

"Did you have a good trip?" She smiled at him.

"Did I have a good trip!" He ran his hands through his hair. "Hell. What kind of question is that?"

"A proper wife always inquires if her husband had a good trip when he comes home."

"It's midnight—or haven't you noticed?"

She raked her eyes over him, and she flushed. "It's hard to notice anything with you undressed like that."

He got up and stalked across the room to pick up

his shorts. There was no need to keep playing with fire. Keeping his back to her and his teeth clenched, he rammed his legs into his shorts. Then he turned around.

"Would you mind explaining what you are doing in my bed?"

"It's *our* bed now."

"*Our* bed?"

"I suppose that jet airplane has damaged your hearing."

"No. I heard you perfectly well the first time. I simply can't believe what I'm hearing."

"It's midnight, Reeve." Belinda gave him another Madonnalike smile. "Do you want to discuss this tonight, or do you want to come to bed and get a good night's sleep so we can be fresh when we talk about it in the morning?"

A good night's sleep? Was the woman out of her mind? How was he supposed to get a good night's sleep with her sharing his bed? Of course, admitting that would be the same as admitting their marriage wasn't all business to him, after all.

Gritting his teeth, he stalked back to bed and climbed in.

"That's a wonderful idea, Belinda." The mattress shifted under his weight, and Belinda rolled a little toward him. When her soft thigh brushed against his he almost jumped out of the bed.

"Oops, sorry," she said, moving her leg a fraction.

"That's perfectly all right." He snapped off the

light and lay rigidly on his side of the bed. "Good night, Belinda."

"Good night, Reeve."

Her silk gown whispered against his legs and her fragrance invaded his senses. He felt his passion rise. One simple movement would put her in his arms. She was his wife, after all.

He forced himself to regain his control. His life was solidly built now on good planning, not emotion.

From her side of the bed came soft stirrings and the gentle rise and fall of her breathing. Out of the darkness, she spoke.

"Sweet dreams, Reeve."

Sweet dreams, indeed. She didn't know the half of it.

A sweet fragrance and the vague awareness of being watched woke Reeve up. He opened his eyes and squinted into the semidarkness. Belinda was sitting on a chair beside his bed, faintly outlined in the gloom and smelling of roses.

"Good morning," she said.

He turned his head toward the windows, expecting to see the morning sun streaming through. Instead he saw only darkness.

"What time is it?" He sat up and immediately regretted it. He had a blinding headache, brought on no doubt by jet lag and a sleepless night with Belinda in his bed.

"Eleven o'clock."

"Eleven o'clock!"

"You needn't shout. I'm not deaf."

"I never sleep until eleven o'clock."

"It's because you're tired from your trip."

"It's those damned curtains over my windows." He vaulted out of bed, intent on getting to the windows to draw his curtains, when the pain in his head stopped him. He clenched his teeth.

"Reeve!" Belinda came out of her chair and caught his arm. Her touch sizzled through him, and he gritted his teeth anew. "Are you all right?"

"Fine," he nearly shouted. Then, forcing himself to moderate his tone, he stepped out of her reach and snapped on the bedside lamp. "I'm fine, Belinda, just a little out of sorts from having overslept."

"I would have awakened you if I had known—"

"It's not your place."

"I'm your wife. I want to help."

He decided it was best not to argue the point at the moment. Instead, he concentrated his attention on his bedroom. It had undergone a change. A crystal vase of roses sat on his bureau. Belinda's pink robe lay across the foot of the bed. Her hairbrush was carelessly tossed onto the bedside table. The door to the closet that had been Sunny's was standing open, and Belinda's clothes hung inside. Her cardboard suitcase sat high upon the closet shelf.

Belinda had moved in.

"Do you mind telling me the meaning of all this?"

He didn't have to elaborate. She was watching him intently.

Belinda drew herself up tall and tried not to show how she was quivering inside. If she ever needed a guardian angel, now was the time, she thought. Reeve was perfectly capable of throwing her out. Not out of the house, of course. But it was highly likely that he would make her move back to her own bedroom. He had certainly made his position clear enough.

And she had gone into the marriage with her eyes open. She couldn't plead innocence on that score. Furthermore, it wouldn't do to get into a battle of wills with Reeve. She was stubborn, but he was implacable. In addition to all that, he must not guess her *real* motive; he must never suspect that she intended to make him fall in love with her.

"It's all very simple, Reeve," she finally said. "You and I know this is only a marriage of convenience, but Quincy and the children do not. Why give any of them cause for suspicion? Unless, of course, you plan to tell Quincy—and perhaps the children—about our little business deal."

"There's no need for anyone to know."

"That's what I thought." She contained her smile. It looked as if she had won round one.

His gaze swept the bedroom once more. Her stamp was everywhere—in the scattered personal belongings, in the sweet aroma of roses, even in the pillow that was still dented from her head. And it wasn't half-bad. In fact, he could get used to having a woman in his bedroom again. There was something heartwarming and altogether peaceful about sharing his most intimate space.

"This doesn't change a thing, of course," he said. "You *do* understand that."

"Yes."

"Good." He reached for his pants, then quirked one eyebrow upward when he saw her standing there watching him. "Enjoying the show, Belinda?"

"Yes." She smiled at him, then added, "I'm not used to seeing a man's body."

"Don't get used to it. I'm early to rise and late to bed. I doubt if you'll be seeing much of my body from now on." He zipped his pants and reached for his shirt. "In fact, I guarantee it."

She nodded and left the bedroom. It wasn't until she was outside the door that she smiled. Then she got so tickled she had to cover her mouth to hold back the sound. She raced down the hallway, shut herself into her old bedroom and collapsed across the bed, giggling.

"Belinda Stubaker Lawrence," she said to herself between gales of laughter. "You've turned into a devious woman."

For the next three days Reeve made excuses to stay late at the office, hoping that by the time he got home she would be fast asleep. Often she was, but that didn't help a bit.

Each night was agony for him. An accidental touch,

an unexpected sigh, set his blood racing and his body quivering. He lay awake warding off her touch.

The tension was telling on him. His work suffered and his temper was short.

Through it all Belinda remained full of grace and good humor. She didn't know much about love—having never experienced it before. But she knew enough about human nature to realize that Reeve was not unaffected by her. If Reeve had nothing except businesslike feelings for her, then why did he react so strongly every time she touched him?

On the fourth morning of their imposed togetherness, she awoke early and leaned on her elbow, watching her husband sleep. Such love for him welled up inside that she had to let it out. She traced his face lightly with her hands, careful not to wake him. "Reeve, my love," she whispered, "my dearest love."

He stirred, moaning softly. *Poor old bear.* He had fought sleep for three nights. She was nobody's fool. She had seen him. And she knew the toll it had taken. Now she guessed that nothing less than a tornado could wake him.

She caressed his face once more, starting at his brow, moving down his cheekbone and ending at his lips. His lips occupied her the longest. Then she placed her head on his shoulder, snuggled close to him and, without meaning to, fell fast asleep.

In a state somewhere between waking and sleeping, Reeve became aware of Belinda's body pressed against his. Involuntarily his hands moved, tracing a hollow here, cupping a curve there. She was incredibly feminine.

He rolled onto his side, pulling her hard up against him. They were a perfect fit. His body came alive, pressing against her, demanding release.

She sighed softly and dug her fingernails into his flesh. The few remnants of sleep fogging his brain vanished. His eyes snapped open, and he awoke with the awful knowledge that he wanted his wife. He loosened his grip, mentally forcing himself to pull away from her; all the same he held on a little while longer, just a little while, but enough to memorize her sweet contours and her intoxicating fragrance.

Then he eased out of bed, being careful not to wake her, and stood gazing down. He was rapidly making a mockery of his businesslike marriage. If many more mornings like this one happened, he wouldn't be able to control himself.

He had been foolish to agree to these sleeping arrangements. Tonight he'd have to talk to her about them.

He reached for his pants. Maybe he wouldn't talk about them at all. Maybe he'd just arrange to move the double bed out and install twin beds.

He pictured Belinda across the room from him on a twin bed. But in his present state, he would want the distance between the beds to be very short. He'd have to install a cast-iron partition between the beds. Then he'd probably be searching for a blowtorch....

* * *

When Belinda awoke, Reeve had already gone. He'd been home almost a week now, and she could see very little progress. The main problem seemed to be that he still saw her mostly as a nanny—in spite of their sleeping arrangements. On those rare occasions when they saw each other long enough to talk, all he ever asked her about was the children. It was high time to change the way he viewed her.

After the children were off to school, she announced to Quincy that she was going on a little outing.

Quincy was immediately skeptical. "What kind of a outin'?"

"I'm going to borrow your car, Quincy, and take the day off to go...sight-seeing."

"If you want to see sights, tell Mr. Reeve. He'll take you."

"Quincy—" Belinda drew herself up tall "—didn't Sunny ever go on outings?"

"Shopping, mostly." Quincy put her hands on her hips. "But she didn't call it no outin'."

"Well, I don't like to shop. I like outings." Acting braver than she felt, Belinda got her purse and sweater out of the hall closet, then turned back to Quincy to get her car keys. "Will you see that the children have their snack when they get home from school?"

"I'll take care of them babies like they was my own. But I smell somethin' rotten here, and it ain't Denmark."

"If I'm not back by five, you may call Mr. Reeve and inform him of my whereabouts."

"And whereabouts would that be?"

"Well...I don't know." Belinda chewed her lower lip. "What's nice to see around here?"

"I likes to go down to Wren, myself. They got the cutest little general store that has 'bout everythin' a body could want to see."

"Tell Reeve I've gone to Wren."

Belinda left before Quincy could say anything else. She wasn't all that sure about her plan in the first place. It wouldn't have taken too much talking to convince her not to go. But she *had* to go. She had to make Reeve see her as a wife who did ordinary things—like go on outings.

She climbed into the car and squared her shoulders. She could drive and she was going to have a peachy time. Then Reeve would sit up and notice.

"She's gone *where?*" Reeve glared at the telephone as if it had struck him.

"Wren," Quincy shouted on the other end of the line. She abhorred phones and always considered it necessary to shout in order to be heard. "Lordy, Mr. Reeve, she tole me to call you if she wasn't back by five, but I didn't want to cause no disturbance—"

"I'll be right home," Reeve said, interrupting her.

Panic hounded Reeve all the way home. It was six-thirty. Belinda had said she would be home by five. And she'd been gone all day. Where was she?

For the sake of the children, he acted as if Belinda had indeed merely gone on a small outing. But by the time he had tucked them into bed, he was almost ready to call the police. Visions of Belinda lying crumpled in a ditch haunted him.

Quincy kept the vigil with him, wringing her hands and moaning. "Oh, Lord, I never shoulda showed her how to drive that car."

"*You* taught her to drive!"

"You don't hafter holler. I ain't deef."

"I'm sorry, Quincy." Reeve ran his hands through his hair. "I didn't know she couldn't drive."

"I guess they's lots of things you dunno 'bout Miss Belinda." Quincy rose on her still old legs. "I'm goin' to bed and I'm gonna pray to the good Lord that no harm come to Miss Belinda. Lordy, she's just a sweet little thing."

Reeve wanted to yell and ram his fist through the wall. Belinda was a sweet woman, a gentle woman—and now he had lost her. He forced himself to act calm.

"Good night, Quincy. Don't worry about a thing. I'm sure she's all right."

After Quincy had gone, Reeve poured himself a good stiff drink of scotch.

At ten-thirty Belinda came strolling in, smiling.

"Hello, Reeve." She tossed the car keys onto the coffee table, then sank onto the sofa and smoothed her stockings.

Relief made Reeve so weak he had to sit. He couldn't even speak for a while, just sat in his chair, staring at the sparkling diamonds along her slim legs and brooding. The urge to hold her was so strong he had to grit his teeth to keep from running to the sofa.

"Quincy told me you'd gone to Wren." He marveled at how steady his voice sounded.

"Yes. I thought I'd have a little outing." She smiled at him. "You don't mind, do you?"

"Of course not. I'm glad to see you enjoying the countryside." He lifted his glass, and they stared at each other over the rim. "In the future, though, please inform me of your plans."

"Certainly." She waited for him to say more, but he didn't. Belinda could have wept. Here she had spent the day off on her own, nearly run over by two trucks and lost as a goose, to boot, and all he could do was ask her to inform him of her plans.

She stood up, head held high and marched from the room. When she was at the door, he called after her. "Where are you going?"

"Does it matter?"

Reeve didn't reply. Belinda hesitated in the doorway, torn between wanting to turn around and run to him and not wanting to make a fool of herself. A few long seconds ticked by, and then she left the den and closed the door. If she was going to be lonesome, she decided she might as well do it by herself.

Reeve didn't realize how hard he was gripping his glass until after she had gone. He stared at the closed door for a long time, then he got up and poured himself another shot of scotch. His nerves were going.

He sat drinking and brooding. Hell, he had never

imagined his marriage would get so complicated. Business wasn't supposed to be like that.

He finished that drink and poured himself another. The third drink took the edge off. A fourth might make things even better. He knew he was drinking too much, but he figured that once wouldn't hurt. Tonight he had earned that right.

While Reeve nursed his scotch, Belinda lay in their lonely bed and stared at the walls. The more she stared the madder she got. Reeve had treated her just like a nanny. She couldn't take it anymore. She didn't know exactly what she was going to do or say, but she was going to do *something*.

Throwing back the covers, she grabbed her robe and flew down the stairs. Her color was high and her belt was dragging on the floor when she flung open the den door.

Reeve was still sitting in his chair, his hair disheveled and his tie askew, holding a glass of scotch.

"You're drinking," she said.

"Is that an accusation?"

Belinda barreled into the room, forgetting every lesson he'd ever taught her on elocution and charm. With her hands wadded into fists, she planted herself in front of his chair.

"Here I've been, gone all day, and you didn't even ask what took me so long!"

Reeve was having the devil of a time maintaining his control. She had no idea how enticing she looked with her robe hanging open that way or she never would have braved his den. If the urge to hold her had been great when she first came home, the passion to kiss her was now like a fire raging through him. He clenched his jaw and kept a tight rein on his control. The scotch made it hard to maintain, though.

"What took you so long, Belinda?"

Things were not going at all the way she wanted them to. Reeve was still as cold and remote as Alaska. She might as well be Belinda Stubaker, back home in Augusta, Georgia.

She thrust out her chin, too furious to think straight.

"What do you care?" she said.

"You are my wife. Therefore, I care."

She stomped away from him and prowled around the room, running her hands over his expensive furniture. When she was behind the sofa, she gripped the back and glared at him.

"You care as much about your Oriental rug as you care about me."

"Forgive me for seeming dense, my dear, but I fail to see how caring enters into our relationship. We had a business deal, remember?" The scotch was blurring his judgment. He knew he wasn't handling her right, but at the moment he didn't know how to do better.

"How could I forget? You remind me at least three times a day."

"Perhaps that's because you need reminding, my dear."

"Stop calling my 'my dear' in that schoolteacher voice. I'm not your dear."

A muscle jumped in Reeve's clenched jaw and he carefully set his scotch on the table. "Belinda, I see no need to continue this discussion."

"Discussion. *Discussion.*" She loosened her grip on the sofa and strode to his chair, her hands on her hips. "This is not a *discussion*—this is a fight."

"I never fight."

"Why do you have to always be so damned civilized?"

"Ladies don't curse."

"Maybe I'm not a lady."

"You are. I made you a lady."

"*You.*" Belinda was in a rage now. It was obvious that Reeve didn't love her, that he would never love her. She had thought that all she wanted was a house to call her own, but now she knew better. What was a house without someone to love waiting inside to make the lonesome blues go away?

Maybe he would turn her out into the street; maybe he would tear up the marriage contract and send her away, but she couldn't stand to be ignored any longer.

She leaned close to his face. "Nobody made me, Reeve Lawrence, and don't you ever forget that."

She was so close he could see the sparks in the center of her eyes and the fine bead of perspiration along her upper lip. He was tempted almost beyond reason. He leaned back and gripped the arms of his chair.

"You're yelling, Belinda."

"You'd yell, too, if you only half knew how to

drive and had gone off to Wren so your husband
would notice you, and then you got lost and nearly
run over by two big trucks, to boot."

"*Nearly run over?*" He grabbed her shoulders so
fast she lost her balance and tumbled into his lap. Her
head snapped back, and she caught at his chest for
balance. There was a great tearing sound as his buttons
popped loose and his shirt came open.

Both of them went very still, then ever so slowly
she wound her hands into the crisp hairs that curled
across his chest. His mouth slammed down on hers,
and he pulled her so close he nearly squeezed the
breath from her.

She wound her arms around his neck as joy coursed
through her. At long last, her husband was noticing
her. Her happiness and the kiss made her so giddy she
almost lost track of everything that was going on.

*Lord, let me hang on to my sanity so I can remem-
ber all this,* she silently prayed.

While his mouth played over hers, his hands seemed
to touch her everywhere. And they were hot where
they touched.

"Reeve," she whispered, when he finally let her up
for air.

"Oh, God. I thought I had lost you." His lips
claimed hers once more, and she felt hot and cold and
happy and scared all at the same time. Feelings such
as she had never known took over. She wanted to get
so close to Reeve that she was under his skin, bur-
rowed into his heart, united with his soul. She felt like

she was turning into another woman altogether. When Reeve flung her robe aside and buried his face in her breasts, she was no longer capable of thought.

"I can't lose you," he said. "I can't. I won't...." His voice was hoarse and almost lost as he pressed his mouth against her soft flesh.

Suddenly he stood up, holding her tightly against his chest. He kicked aside her robe and strode from the den.

"Reeve?" she whispered. "Reeve?"

He didn't answer. His footsteps echoed on the marble tiles as he marched across the hall toward the staircase. Belinda held on, her heart hammering so hard she could barely breathe.

When Reeve reached his bedroom, he plunged through the door, then kicked it shut. He hadn't said a word on his relentless march up the stairs. His face was so fierce Belinda couldn't have looked at it if she hadn't been seeing him through the eyes of love.

The bed loomed before them, seeming twice as big as when she had left it. The single lamp she'd left burning cast a bright glow across the covers. Reeve strode straight to the bed. He gazed at her a moment, one tight muscle twitching in his clenched jaw. Then he dropped her onto the bed. She bounced once and settled in a heap of silk.

Staring down at her with eyes gone as dark as doom, Reeve stripped off his clothes and flung them aside. Belinda wet her lips with her tongue. Nervous perspiration popped out across her brow, and she brushed her heavy hair aside.

When Reeve was as magnificently naked as one of the Greek statues he'd shown her in the art books, he bent over her, his jaw still tight. "Do you have any idea how much I want you?" His voice made her shiver. "Do you know how many times I've wanted to have you like this, stretched across my bed waiting for me?" The scent of scotch was strong on his breath, but she didn't turn away. He was the man she loved, and he would never hurt her. Of that she was certain.

He poised above her, propping himself with his hands on either side of her shoulders. A battle waged in his face, then suddenly he caught her gown where it dipped low across her breasts and pulled it aside. The fabric parted with a small tearing sound, and she lay before him as smooth and exposed as a freshly blooming flower.

The last of his control shattered. He covered her with his hands, his mouth, his body. For a moment she was still and quivering, then she turned liquid and pliant under him. All the things she had made him dream of came true. All the places he had longed to touch were his at last. He moved his hands over her in a way as old as time, and yet each touch, each caress, felt new—as if it had just been invented for this moment. Wonder and joy were reborn in him, and a passion such as he had never known, a passion that could no longer be denied.

Heady with scotch and desperate with desire, he

kissed and caressed until he could bear the waiting no more.

With a great cry he sought the final release. She, too, cried out, but he was past hearing. He had become a summer storm, raging through soft warm pastures and fragrant fields of flowers.

Passions so long denied were not easily spent. Lost in the mystery of Belinda, oblivious to everything except the sweet hot pleasure that coursed through him, Reeve maintained his course and spent his love until he lay exhausted across his wife.

His breath came in harsh gasps. It was a while before he could speak. He drew a steadying breath and rolled to his side. Belinda lay unmoving. He reached out and touched her face. It was dripping with sweat.

"Belinda?" He leaned onto his elbows. It wasn't sweat on her face, it was tears. "Oh, my God..." He pushed her damp hair back from her forehead. She merely gazed at him with eyes as big as twin harvest moons. "Belinda?"

She turned her face aside.

Reeve died inside. He got off the bed and reached for his pants. With his back to her, he dressed quickly. There was no sound from the bed.

When he was fully dressed he turned for one last look at Belinda. She was huddled in the middle of the bed like a fallen flower, her torn gown spread, petal-like, around her.

With his heart heavy, he left the room, closing the door quietly behind him. He made his mind a careful blank until he was outside the house, standing in the midst of his rose garden. The fragrance brought Belinda sharply back to his mind, and he pictured her on the bed as he had last seen her, flushed, disheveled and teary-eyed.

The truth struck him with such force it nearly brought him to his knees. Belinda was a virgin. In the throes of passion and under the influence of the scotch, he had not noticed. But now, sane and sober in his rose garden, he replayed the scene in his mind—her nervousness, her stiffness, that small cry that he had thought to be passion. He lowered his face to his hands and groaned. What he had done to her was unspeakable beyond all enduring. There was no way he could restore what he had taken from her. His only consolation was that she was his wife.

His wife. He remembered the vows they had exchanged in this same rose garden. *To love and to cherish.* In a moment of great clarity, Reeve understood that he loved Belinda, had always loved Belinda, *would* always love her. Oh, God, why had he been so slow to know?

He loved his wife, and now it was too late.

He sank onto the stone bench beside his late-blooming peace roses. He welcomed the cold stone. He wanted punishment for his sins, for surely there was no atonement.

Reeve stayed on the stone bench, lost in pity for himself and his wife, until his natural coping mechanisms fell back into place. He was a businessman. It was time for him to take a businesslike look at his problems.

Number one: he had been lying to himself about his reasons for a marriage of convenience. It was true that he had wanted permanence in his life, but it was also true that he had been afraid of loving her. He had seen a glimmer of that truth this evening when she didn't come home. He had loved and lost once, and he hadn't wanted to love and lose again. That was all beside the point now. At long last he could admit to himself that he loved her.

Number two: how could he convince her of his love?

With a speed born of purpose, Reeve went back inside and closeted himself in his study. Sleep didn't matter anymore. What mattered was laying a plan for winning his wife.

Reeve was gone when Belinda awoke the next morning. She had known he would be. Wearily she dragged herself out of bed and into the bathroom. She looked the way she felt—like a frazzled kitten left too long in the rain. She draped a towel over the mirror so she wouldn't see herself, then drew a hot bath.

Bathtub therapy. She doubted it would work this time. Her husband didn't love her. What had happened last night in his bed hasn't been love; it had been lust. Belinda Stubaker Lawrence wasn't born yesterday. What she didn't know about sex could fill an ocean or two, but she did know it wasn't all it was cracked up to be. Of course, that could have all been her fault.

She pressed her head back against the cold tiles and closed her eyes. Nothing had changed, and nothing was going to change. Maybe after her bath she'd pack her things and leave. There was always another town waiting for her somewhere.

"Belinda?"

Her eyes snapped open. Reeve was squatting beside the tub, smiling at her. Instinctively she covered her breasts with the washcloth.

"I thought you had gone."

"I did for a while. I had things to do." He had dark circles under his eyes and the shadow of a beard on his face. It looked as if he hadn't even shaved this morning. What was the world coming to?

"Business?" She was surprised she could even speak. After last night, she hadn't thought she could look at him again, let alone talk to him.

"No, not business." Smiling, he reached for her hand and lifted it to his lips, soap bubbles and all. She figured she must be hallucinating. He spent considerable time kissing her hand, then he smiled at her again. "Not business at all, my love."

My love? Now she knew she was dreaming. The bathwater was beginning to get cold, but she didn't notice. All she could see was her husband, looking at her like a lover. Her heart kicked hard against her ribs.

"What, then?"

"I had to apologize, Belinda, for last night."

"Well..." She bit her lip until she could taste blood. Reeve Lawrence always had a way of making her forget her purpose. Here she was, all set to pack her bags, no matter what sort of deal she had made with him, and here he was, all gentle and precious, squatting beside her tub making her feel like a cherished rose.

He gently touched her lips. "Don't say anything else, love. You don't have to talk, just listen."

She nodded.

"I had no idea you were innocent," he said first.

"I told you nobody had ever picked my plums," she blurted.

"I know you did. I guess all I heard that day was how you had left St. Louis with Charlie Crocket. Belinda, forgive me—I assumed you had lived with him."

"I did. Just like I lived with you—until last night."

"That won't happen again, Belinda. I promise you."

She thought she was going to cry. How many more ways was Reeve going to think up to let her know she was not a wife to him? She dredged her pride from the depths of her soul and lifted her chin.

"No," she said. "It won't. I'm leaving."

"*Leaving!*" His roar of outrage echoed around the bathroom, but to her credit, Belinda didn't even flinch. But she had an implacable expression on her face that let him know in no uncertain terms that she meant what she'd said.

Reeve stood up and looked down at her. What he wanted to do was lift her from the tub, carry her to his bed and make slow sweet love to her. What he *must* do was get himself back under control enough to keep her from leaving.

"I'm sorry, Belinda. I didn't mean to shout."

"I guess you didn't expect me to leave."

"No. I didn't." He sat on the edge of the tub and caught her hand. "Belinda, my behavior last night was inexcusable, but if you'll give me two weeks, I'll try to make it all up to you."

"Two weeks?"

"That's all I ask. If at the end of two weeks you still want to leave, I won't try to stop you."

"What about our marriage contract?"

"I'll have it set aside."

She considered his request for a long, long time. She didn't want to leave, not now, not ever. And yet, loving Reeve and knowing he would never love her, how could she stay?

"Belinda..." he urged softly.

At that moment she knew she couldn't leave. Love was worth any risk. Who knew what she might accomplish in two weeks? She might even get her husband to love her. Miracles did happen.

"Two weeks," she said. "I promise."

"Deal."

He leaned down and pressed his lips against her wet cheek, then stood up to leave. She sank back into her now-cold water. There was no need to get out of the tub yet. The children were at school, and Reeve would be at his office.

She closed her eyes and shivered. Just suppose she had last night to do all over again. Suppose Reeve had explained all the ways of love to her and given her enough time to get used to things. Images played through her mind, and she sighed. Parts of last night had been wonderful. She wished for a second chance, to know if *all* of it could have been wonderful.

"Belinda Stubaker Lawrence," she lectured herself as she got out of the tub, "since when have you waited for second chances? Do you think your own private Santa Claus is going to hand things to you on a silver platter?"

Her spirits restored, she dressed carefully and started down the stairs. She was born fighting for the things she wanted, and the next two weeks she would wage a full-scale battle. But first, she'd try to find out what the opposite camp was up to.

After he left the bathroom, Reeve took time to place two phone calls, then he stationed himself at the end of the staircase, waiting. Eventually she would come that way, and he wanted to be there to watch her descent. One of the things he loved most about Belinda was the elegant way she descended a staircase.

He loved her. Why hadn't he told her so in the bathroom? He guessed it would take him a while to get used to the idea himself. Anyway, she wouldn't have believed him. He had to *show* her his love before he declared it.

All he had ever shown her was that he was the boss and she was the nanny. That couldn't be changed overnight.

He heard a noise at the top of the staircase and looked up. There she was, poised like a queen, her legs sparkling with rhinestone hearts. His breath actually caught in his throat, and it took him a while to be able to breathe properly.

If he lived to be a hundred he would never get enough of seeing Belinda in her wonderful stockings.

She spotted him and hesitated, then gave him a smile and began to come down the stairs. She was a polished and elegant woman and yet she was still the same refreshing woman who had walked sideways down the street lugging her cardboard suitcase. Natural charm and beauty had always been hers.

He kept his eyes on hers until she was even with him, standing on the second step.

"I thought you would be gone to the office," she said.

"I'll be conducting business from the house for the next two weeks."

She studied him, trying to guess his purpose. But as always, Reeve was unreadable. "In that case, I'll be certain not to disturb you."

She came the rest of the way down the stairs and started to walk past him. He caught her arm and gently stopped her.

"Don't go, Belinda...please."

"Since you put it so nicely, and since you are my husband, I'm bound to obey."

"You look especially pretty today."

"Thank you. I dressed for you."

Hope sprang in him. "You did?"

"Yes. I know you like me in red."

"I like you in all colors."

They considered each other for a while. Belinda was the first to look away.

"Belinda—" Reeve touched one cheek with the back of his hand and gently turned her to face him "—is red still your favorite color?"

"Yes." The way he was rubbing his hand against her cheek, he could have asked if mud-brown was her favorite color and she'd have agreed. She covered his hand with hers. "I like that."

"You do?"

"Yes."

They stayed that way—with his hand on her cheek and her hand covering his—until the sound of the doorbell tore them apart. Belinda was jumpy with nerves. She started toward the door, then remembered that this was Reeve's house and he was home. She stopped halfway to the door and looked at him over her shoulder.

"Would you get that, please?" he asked.

Belinda opened the door to a young man holding his hat and a small package.

"Delivery for Mrs. Reeve Lawrence."

"For me?"

"Are you Mrs. Lawrence?"

Belinda was too surprised to answer. Instead she twisted her head to look at Reeve. He strode forward and put his arm lightly around her shoulders.

"She is," he said.

The young man handed her the package, then set his cap back on his head and tipped it at a jaunty angle. "Somebody must like you an awful lot to be giving you a birthday present like that."

"It's not my birthday."

"Every day for the next two weeks is going to be your birthday, Belinda," said Reeve. "I promise you that."

The delivery boy grinned, then left the porch, whistling. Belinda stood in the open doorway, staring at the small package in her hand.

"Aren't you going to open it?" Reeve asked.

She pulled the red ribbon off, being careful not to break it. Then she took the same care with the bright striped paper.

"I like the wrappings."

Reeve chuckled. "So I see."

By the time she finally opened the box, he could barely contain his excitement. He hadn't felt this young and giddy in years.

"Two keys?" Belinda lifted the key chain, inspecting it and the keys on all sides. "Well—" she gave him a perky smile "—that's lovely, Reeve. Thank you."

"Aren't you even going to ask what the keys fit into?"

"Some people decorate with keys—hang them on the wall and all that."

"Come with me." Reeve took her hand and led her down the driveway. Parked in front of their house was a bright red car, as square and sturdy as a box, but bright red, nonetheless.

"For you, Belinda."

"A car!"

"It's all yours, Mrs. Lawrence."

"Boy, when you apologize you really do it with style." She walked around the car, running her hands over the shiny paint, leaning down to admire the leather seats through the window.

"Do you like it?"

"It's the finest gift anybody ever gave me." She looked at the car one last time—with regret. Then she handed the keys to Reeve. "I can't take it."

"You can't take it?"

"Has your hearing done bad? That's what I said."

Reeve suddenly remembered how stubborn she had been about the clothes. "If you don't like the color or the style, we can take it back right now and get something different."

"It's not that." Belinda bit her lips, then she plunged in and told him the truth. "I was so scared down there in Wren, I nearly passed out. There I was, off in a part of the country I didn't know trying to drive a car when I barely had my license."

She pressed the keys into his hand once more. "Thank you just the same, Reeve, but I've given up driving. I was terrible at it."

Reeve smiled. "That's because you had the wrong teacher."

"Quincy was very patient."

"But hardly an expert."

Reeve took the keys from her and unlocked the door. "Come inside, love. Today you're going to get a lesson from a *real* teacher."

"Do you mean that? You're going to help me with driving?" She climbed into the car and ran her hands over the leather.

Reeve slid into the driver's seat. "For the next two weeks I'm going to devote myself to you."

Her color high, she gave him a shy smile. He reached for her hand across the smooth expanse of leather, then lifted it to his lips. She knew she had to do something quick or she would be back to the same old Belinda, blown around like a dandelion by the whims of the man she loved. She pulled her hand out of his grasp and placed it demurely in her lap. *This* time she wasn't going to tumble into his arms without knowing what the future held. This time she was going to be a different Belinda Stubaker Lawrence—if she could get her heart to wait.

She reached for the door handle. "This car is just peachy, Reeve. And I do thank you, but I can't stick around. I have lots of things to do, and before you know it the children will be home from school, hungry as two little bears.''

"Stay, Belinda." She faced him, her chin stubborn. "Please," he added. "The children won't be home this afternoon. I called Sunny's parents. Betsy and Mark and Quincy are spending the weekend with the Wentworths."

"Well..."

While she hesitated, Reeve reached across her and fastened her seat belt.

"The first thing you should learn about driving a car is to fasten your seat belt."

Teaching always brought out the best in Reeve. Belinda gave him a smart little salute and smiled. "Yes, master."

Reeve settled back behind the wheel. "Are you ready for your first lesson, Belinda?"

"Carry on, Teach."

Reeve drove her into the country, stopping long enough to pick up some food for a picnic. They spent a glorious day together. Reeve was patient and kind and gentle. Under his expert tutelage, Belinda lost her fear of the car. And she almost lost her resolve. Reeve was as attentive as a storybook hero, and she was ready to believe he really did love her. The only problem was he hadn't said a thing about love.

"Rome wasn't built in a day," she mumbled to herself on the way home.

"What?"

"I said it would be nice to nap in the hay."

He grinned at her. "I'll have to remember that."

It was late by the time they returned home. The house was dark and deserted.

Reeve took Belinda's arm and led her inside. He took her coat and hung it in the hall closet, and with the chandelier blazing brightly down upon them she looked at the man who was her husband.

He was watching her in a way that made her think he might be going to have her for dinner. She shivered. Oh, Lordy, how did a woman whose experience extended to the likes of Charlie Crocket deal with a man like Reeve Lawrence? She felt like David going up against Goliath—without a sling. Why had she ever imagined she could win his love, let alone hold it? If she lived to be a hundred she would never understand all the mountains and valleys and rivers of his soul. He was the most complex man she had ever met—and the most exciting.

She pressed her hands together over her heart. He hadn't let up on that intense look that turned her body to flames. "Belinda—" he placed one hand on her cheek "—are you all right?"

"Yes. I'm..." She paused, caught up in the burning look of his eyes. Finally she was able to look away. "I'm tired, I guess. I think I'll just go on up to bed."

"At six o'clock?"

"Well...I'm going to...read. Yes, that's it. I'm going to read in bed until I fall asleep."

"In that case..." His eyes darkened as he cupped her face with his hands.

"What are you doing?" she whispered.

"Giving you a good-night kiss. You *are* my wife."

His lips were exquisitely tender. Belinda thought she had actually become a dandelion and was floating off across the fields looking for a place to land. Fortunately for her, when Reeve finished the kiss, she landed on her feet. She even managed a dignified exit.

"Good night, Reeve." She climbed the staircase the best way she could, knowing he was watching her. When she got to the top, she pressed one hand over her heart and headed down the hall. She had to get to a bed before she collapsed. The only trouble was which bed?

When she came to the two doorways, she hesitated only a moment. There was no way she would go back into Reeve's bedroom—not until she knew how things stood.

She pushed open her bedroom door and went inside. It didn't matter a whit to her that all her things were now in Reeve's room. She would wrap herself in the sheet; she'd wrap herself in a towel. By George, Belinda Stubaker Lawrence was somebody—somebody who deserved to be loved. And until she could figure out a way to make that happen, she would not darken his doorway.

After her bath, she scouted all the closets and drawers looking for a scrap of clothing she might have left behind. But it was no use. When she and Quincy had packed all her things, they had been very thorough.

There was not a single stitch to show that she had ever occupied the blue-and-cream bedroom.

"Never mind," she said. Then she climbed into bed naked and sat staring at the door. She felt rather cowardly. To top things off, she had forgotten to get a book. How was she ever going to pass the time until she got sleepy?

She sat that way for forty-five minutes, waiting and listening. She loved this house to distraction. The only trouble was it was so well built she couldn't hear a darned thing.

A soft tapping came at her door. Before she could say a word, it eased open. "Belinda?"

Reeve stood in the doorway, his eyes bright and his hands carrying a tray. "May I come in?"

"Certainly." She was so absorbed in watching him that she forgot her nakedness until he was standing over her.

"You look fetching without your clothes, my love."

She pulled the covers up to her chin. She would die before she would admit to not wanting to go back into his bedroom to get her nightgown.

"It's such a lovely evening I thought I'd give my skin a breather."

"I approve."

He hid his chuckle by turning his back to her and setting the tray on the bedside table. "You forgot dinner, so I made you a small meal." He turned back to her. "I also brought you a book." He was holding a copy of love sonnets by Elizabeth Barrett Browning.

"Thank you." She reached for the volume, and he caught her hand.

"Belinda..." The bed sank under his weight as he sat down. Her heart kicked up such a rhythm she thought she might quit breathing. He reached up and smoothed her hair, staring deeply into her eyes. She held her breath, waiting. She felt just like a princess in a fairy tale. This was the moment when the hero leaned over the princess and declared his undying love.

"Yes?" she whispered.

She waited so long she thought she heard the minutes cracking into pieces and falling about the floor.

"When you're ready to come to my bed, I'll be waiting," he said. Then he stood up and left.

She sat there looking at the closed door. Well, dammit. That man was enough to drive her to curse.

Reeve stood outside her door, holding the doorknob. What in the devil was the matter with him? He had thought he could stick to his plan of winning her love, then declaring it. But when he was staring down at her all tousled and dreamy-eyed in her bed, every logical thought went out of his head. He could barely remember what he had said to her. Something about waiting for her in his bed. As if last night weren't enough, he'd added insult to injury.

He couldn't seem to keep his thoughts focused, but he supposed that was what happened when a hard-nosed businessman who had resisted love for years finally took a fall. Not only had he lost all his courting skills, he had lost all his control.

Tomorrow he'd do better.

The next morning Reeve waited for Belinda at the foot of the staircase. During the sleepless night he had made a new resolution. Two weeks be damned. Good things were worth waiting for, that was true, but he had never been the kind of man who stretched out a deal. Today was his day to close the deal with Belinda.

When she finally appeared she was wearing yesterday's dress. He smiled. One of the things he loved about her was her strong will. He knew she wouldn't go back into his bedroom, even if she had to wear that same dress every day for a week. And he knew why.

His smile broadened. After today, all that would change.

"Good morning, my love. Sleep well?"

"Yes." He knew she was lying by the way she turned her eyes away from him ever so briefly.

"Great. Then you're up to another surprise."

With one hand on the railing, she paused. "Gee, with all these gifts, I'm beginning to feel like a visiting dignitary."

"What I want you to feel like is a wife."

She brought her gaze to his, but said nothing. He reached for her hand and led her onto the front porch. It was transformed. Red geraniums were everywhere. Two huge urns flanked the doorway; hanging baskets swung in the early-fall breeze, and pots of all sizes were banked artfully around two enormous rocking chairs.

"Reeve!" Belinda ran around the porch, stopping to sniff a red bloom, pausing to admire a hanging basket, laughing and crying at the same time. When she was even with the rocking chairs, she faced him. "What does this mean?"

"It means I love you."

She sank slowly into one of the chairs. Reeve knelt at her side.

"I hadn't meant to tell you like this..."

"I don't know why not. This is the most wonderful surprise in the whole world. These pots of geraniums and these rockers tell me more about how you feel than..." She squeezed her hands together over her lap, and two big tears splashed down her cheeks.

"Than the car, Belinda?"

"Yes. Than the car...and all the clothes and all the finery in the world." She bent over and caught his face between her hands. "Oh, Reeve, you know how I've always wanted a little house to call my own with red geraniums on the front porch."

"Will a big house do just as well?" Another tear inched down her cheek. Reeve reached up and tenderly brushed it aside. "I love you, Belinda. I guess I've loved you from the start. I just didn't know how to tell you."

She pressed her cheek against his. "I've been loving you since the beginning of time. All these years I've been going from place to place, searching for a little house, sometimes even searching for a man to live in it with me...." She wiped her face and laughed. "And here I end up in Tupelo, Mississippi. Why, I reckon God must have had you in mind for me all along."

Reeve lifted her off the rocking chair, then sat back down in it with her in his lap. "How do you feel about making this a *real* marriage, Belinda?"

"In my heart it has always been a real marriage."

With the scent of geraniums sweet around them and the fall breezes playing across the porch, Reeve kissed his wife. She was rosy-cheeked and glowing when they drew apart.

Reeve set the rocker into motion and held her close against his chest, wondering how he'd ever gotten so lucky.

"Reeve?" She lifted her head to look at him.

"Hmm?"

"There's something I've been wondering."

"Yes?"

"Did you plan to court me for two weeks?"

"Indeed, I did."

"Now that I've already decided to stay, what do you think we'll do for the next two weeks?"

He chuckled. "We'll think of something, Belinda."

"I'm thinking of another lesson."

"A driving lesson?"

"No. Not that." She blushed. Reeve stilled the rocking chair. "About the other night, Reeve... Do you think we might try that again? I don't think I got it right the first time."

All the love and passion and mystery of marriage rose between them as they gazed into each other's eyes. Then Reeve rose from the rocking chair and carried his bride inside the house and up the staircase.

When they lay together upon his bed, he said, "We'll practice until we get this right."

Epilogue

Belinda wanted everything to be perfect for Mark's high school graduation party.

She raced through the house, making sure that all the party streamers were hung and all the food was spread on the table. Baby Jennifer and four-year-old Matthew were napping in the nursery, and Betsy had taken the nine-year-old twins, Sammy and Sarah, to a matinee so they wouldn't be underfoot. Quincy had bullied Rosemond, the new housekeeper, into taking her shopping for a proper graduation dress.

"I ain't wearin' nothin' but purple," she had said. "One of my babies is gettin' graduated and I feels like royalty. I'm wearin' a purple dress and that's that."

Belinda had the house all to herself. She made one last inspection, then went out to the front porch and sat down in one of the rockers. The scent of geraniums wafted around her. She leaned back and closed her eyes.

"Napping, my love?"

She looked up and there was her husband, as gloriously handsome and appealing as he had been the first day she had met him.

"Just resting my eyes. You know I'm never tired."

"I know." Chuckling, he sat down in the rocking chair beside her and took her hand.

"Where is everybody?"

"Matthew and Jennifer are napping. Everyone else has gone."

"Hmm. That gives us two hours till the party." He scooped her in his arms and started into the house, smiling down at her. "Do you have any idea how we might occupy ourselves during that time, my love?"

She wrapped her arms around him and nuzzled his neck as he started up the stairs. "I was thinking of another lesson. I still don't think I've got it right."

Laughing, Reeve carried her into the bedroom and kicked the door shut.

"I'm so glad I married a woman who understands the benefit of continuing education."

* * * * * *

SPECIAL EDITION

Stories of love and life, these powerful novels are tales that you can identify with—romances with "something special" added in!

Fall in love with the stories of authors such as **Nora Roberts, Diana Palmer, Ginna Gray** and many more of your special favorites—as well as wonderful new voices!

Special Edition brings you entertainment for the heart!

If you've got the time...
We've got the
INTIMATE MOMENTS

Passion. Suspense. Desire. Drama. Enter a world
that's larger than life, where men and women
overcome life's greatest odds for the ultimate
prize: love. Nonstop excitement is closer than you
think...in Silhouette Intimate Moments!

WAYS TO UNEXPECTEDLY MEET MR. RIGHT:

♡ *Go out with the sexy-sounding stranger your daughter secretly set you up with through a personal ad.*

♡ *RSVP yes to a wedding invitation—soon it might be your turn to say "I do!"*

♡ *Receive a marriage proposal by mail— from a man you've never met....*

These are just a few of the unexpected ways that written communication leads to love in Silhouette Yours Truly.

Each month, look for two fast-paced, fun and flirtatious Yours Truly novels (with entertaining treats and sneak previews in the back pages) by some of your favorite authors—and some who are sure to become favorites.

YOURS TRULY™:

Love—when you least expect it!

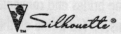

Silhouette®

YT-GEN

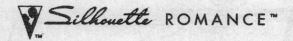

What's a single dad to do when he needs a wife by next Thursday?

Who's a confirmed bachelor to call when he finds a baby on his doorstep?

How does a plain Jane in love with her gorgeous boss get him to notice her?

From classic love stories to romantic comedies to emotional heart tuggers, **Silhouette Romance** offers six irresistible novels every month by some of your favorite authors! Such as...beloved bestsellers **Diana Palmer, Annette Broadrick, Suzanne Carey, Elizabeth August** and **Marie Ferrarella**, to name just a few—and some sure to become favorites!

Fabulous Fathers...Bundles of Joy...Miniseries... Months of blushing brides and convenient weddings... Holiday celebrations... You'll find all this and much more in **Silhouette Romance**—always emotional, always enjoyable, always about love!

SILHOUETTE® Desire®

Do you want...

Dangerously handsome heroes

Evocative, everlasting love stories

Sizzling and tantalizing sensuality

Incredibly sexy miniseries like **MAN OF THE MONTH**

Red-hot romance

Enticing entertainment that can't be beat!

You'll find all of this, and much *more* each and every month in **SILHOUETTE DESIRE**. Don't miss these unforgettable love stories by some of romance's hottest authors. Silhouette Desire—where your fantasies will always come true....